SmartRats

THOMAS BAIRD

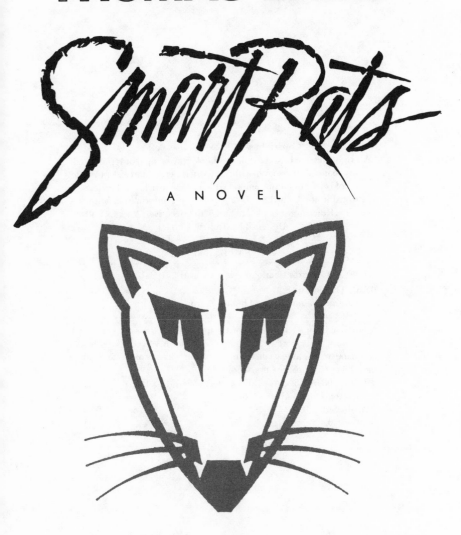

Smart Rats

A NOVEL

Harper & Row, Publishers

Library of Congress Cataloging-in-Publication Data
Baird, Thomas, date
   Smart rats : a novel / by Thomas Baird.
      p.   cm.
   Summary: In a terrifying near future in which the wasteland Earth
can no longer support all its human population, a seventeen-year-old
is endangered by a new edict calling for the relocation of one child
from every two-progeny household.
   ISBN 0-06-020364-1. — ISBN 0-06-020365-X (lib. bdg.)
   [1. Science fiction.]   I. Title.
PZ7.B166Sm   1990   90-4140
[Fic]—dc20   CIP
                                                                  AC

This book is dedicated to the passenger pigeon, the great blue whale, the mountain gorilla, the rain forests of the Amazon and Alaska, Prince William Sound, the Adriatic, and all the other species and places that mankind has destroyed or is destroying. Retribution for our greed and folly cannot long be delayed, and when the reckoning comes, some will pay more than others.

THE
NEW
PROGRAM

1

A few minutes before the hour, Lieutenant Lyman Lindgren, a handsome young officer smartly turned out in the dress uniform of the NORSEC Law Enforcement Corps, jumped up on a portable aluminum podium and braced the tip of his command baton against the gold stripe that ran down his right leg. His detachment of corpsmen, fully armed, was in riot deploy. The prison van waited, prisoners and their guards still inside. The contaminators stood in front of their orange-striped truck. Next to the podium, the flag of the Council of NORSEC—a white outline of New England and the Middle Atlantic States against a blue background—barely stirred in the warm morning air. The rationed citizens had gathered around the podium, whispering to each other.

At eight A.M. sharp, Lindgren signaled his sergeant to call for silence, then solemnly declared, "The procedures to which Lewis and Mary Pratt and their progeny, Emily and Samuel, have been sentenced will now begin. Bring the prisoners forward."

Corpsmen pulled the four prisoners out of the prison van and led them—by shining plastic cords attached to wide blue plastic collars that held their heads unnaturally erect—to a space in front of the podium. Two of the prisoners, a man and woman, were in their late forties or early fifties. Two were younger, a female of about twenty-three and a male of perhaps seventeen. All wore watches on both wrists; otherwise they were naked.

Lieutenant Lindgren reviewed their appearance, his pale-blue eyes pitiless beneath the bill of his cap. Lewis Pratt had some cuts on his face and arms, new since the day before. Mary Pratt, his wife, who was trembling, was bruised on her legs. Their son, Sam, had a crisscross of soft welts on his back and sides. Their guards had been practicing.

"I will now read aloud the pertinent parts of the sentence handed down by the magistrate who sat in judgment in this case," Lindgren said. "Quote:

" 'I hereby decree that the said Pratt family, having confessed and been found guilty as accused of the crime of Trade and Barter, shall be stripped of all the privileges of rationed citizenship, and their rations disks be destroyed. Furthermore, I decree that their place of residence, in Mile Seven, Local Center Fourteen of the Northeast Sector of the North American Jurisdiction (hereafter to be known as NORSEC), shall be contaminated, along with all their personal possessions therein.

" 'I further decree that they, the condemned, shall be present when the contamination procedure is executed, and shall be made to observe it. Evidence of their crimes shall, moreover, be exhibited. At least one member of each domestic unit from the mile in which they resided shall be present to observe the procedure and be instructed in the case.' "

Lieutenant Lindgren lowered the document. "Will the milemaster of this mile identify himself?"

A man of medium height, who'd been standing between a boy the same age as Samuel Pratt and a much younger girl, dropped the girl's hand and stepped forward. "I am the milemaster of Mile Seven of Local Center Fourteen," he said, almost inaudibly.

"Speak up. Your name?"

"Arthur Grayson."

"Is at least one member of each domestic unit in this mile present, as ordered by the magistrate?" Lindgren asked.

"No, sir. One domestic unit is not represented."

"You will be held responsible for this irregularity."

"Please, sir. Please let me explain," the milemaster said. "Please." He tried to touch Lindgren's knee in supplication, but the sergeant blocked him. "Amos Barnard was killed two weeks ago. Gloria, his wife, has just had their first baby."

"She should have come and brought the baby."

"She only had him yesterday, sir."

"Have you written an explanation of these circumstances?" Grayson nodded and held out a piece of paper. "Give it to the sergeant. Now, have you an official tally of the other domestic units?" Grayson handed the sergeant another piece of paper, then eased himself backward and took the girl's hand again. "I will attach the documents to the file of these procedures, for later review and evaluation," Lindgren said. He raised his voice. "You have heard the sentence?" The assembled citizens murmured. "And you understand the reasons for it? That Pratt, formerly a supervisor at the dry-goods distribution outlet at your center, stole wristwatches from the inventory of the outlet and illegally traded them for other goods, and that he did this with the knowledge and encouragement of his wife, and also that he gave wristwatches to her and to his children who are, under the laws of NORSEC, held culpable? All this you understand?" There was another murmur.

Lindgren signaled with his baton, whereupon a corpsman wearing the blue gloves of NORSEC approached the Pratts. While the corpsman who stood behind Lewis Pratt steadied his prisoner, the other slapped Pratt on both sides of his face. He then struck wife, daughter, and son in the same way.

"That is to signify that there is no place they can turn in hope of mercy," the lieutenant explained to the citizens.

The youth with the milemaster looked around and seemed about to walk away; however, the milemaster seized his arm and whispered to him, and he stayed in his place.

"Prisoners, raise your arms," Lindgren commanded. "You see on their wrists the watches they were trading and bartering. To possess them they have forfeited their rights as rationed citizens. Sergeant, move the prisoners to the van."

As Sam Pratt, who was the last in line, passed in front of the young girl who was with the milemaster, she put out a foot just far enough to trip him, then drew the foot back so quickly almost nobody noticed.

Sam fell to his knees.

Lindgren signaled the sergeant, who touched his electric prod to the welts on Sam's naked flank. Sam screamed and jerked and clutched his side. "Move him along, move him along," Lindgren said. The sergeant prodded Sam repeatedly. Screaming and screaming, Sam scrambled to the prison van, where he collapsed, face down.

"Get on your feet! Observe the procedure as ordered," Lindgren said. "I give you to the count of five. Sergeant, stand by. One. Two." Sam tried again but flopped back to the ground. His father strained at his collar and cord to try to get to Sam and help him, but the guard restrained him. "Three. Four." Sam struggled to his knees. "Not good enough," Lindgren said. "Sergeant—" Sam managed to stand.

"That's better," Lindgren said. "Contaminators, proceed."

The contaminators—two men, two women—put on their special clothing and headgear, then took canisters and sprays and entered the red-sided house that had belonged to the Pratts. A short while later they emerged. One of them nailed shut the front door, while the others posted notices on the walls and windows.

DANGER	DANGER
DESTRON	
DANGER	DANGER

After they'd got out of their special clothing, they put up a sign in front of the house.

```
┌─────────────────────────────────────────────┐
│               OFF LIMITS                      │
│   DO NOT APPROACH OR ENTER THESE              │
│              PREMISES:                        │
│   THEY HAVE BEEN CONDEMNED AND                │
│           CONTAMINATED                        │
│   BY ORDER OF THE COUNCIL OF NORSEC           │
│               OFF LIMITS                      │
└─────────────────────────────────────────────┘
```

Lindgren said, "Those signs mean what they say. In case there are any thieves present, let me remind you that many of the people who get sent to the Center for Incurables are Destron-exposure cases. The cartilage in their joints has rotted out. Or they're gasping for breath. Or raving mad. So fair warning."

He went on reading from the sentence. " 'When this will have been done, the condemned shall be taken to the NORSEC Deportation Center for transshipment to the penal islands, and shall be exhibited along the way, at such local centers as the officer in charge may deem convenient, as an example to other rationed citizens.

" 'These things I decree, by the authority vested in me by the Council of NORSEC.' "

Lindgren folded the document. He waited while the guards pushed the Pratts into the prison van, then said, "The contamination and exhibition procedures are hereby completed." He looked around at the rationed citizens. "You may disperse." He strode off to the car that was waiting for him.

Meanwhile, the youth who was with Milemaster Grayson had moved close to the van. When young Sam Pratt looked in his direction, the youth scratched the back of his head. As he was lowering his hand, he curled his thumb up against his middle fingers and scratched them together rapidly, as if they were gnawing on something.

Sam, if he saw the gesture, was beyond giving any acknowledgment.

2

When he reached the top of the ridge and could see the Connecticut River winding through its valley ahead, Laddie Grayson stopped to cool down.

It was early September, so the worst months were over. The morning had turned out fairly nice, hot but not too humid for a change. The sun was bright, but the sunrise radio summary Laddie and his father had listened to before going off with his sister, Greta, to the Pratt contamination procedure had classified all of NOR-SEC "low risk." Exposure to solar radiation, even between nine and three, was statistically acceptable. Laddie tucked his cap under his belt, took off his shirt and tied it to the handlebars of his bike, and enjoyed the breeze.

Not that the statisticians didn't make mistakes. Computational errors, they called it. Their errors were your skin cancer.

Laddie got out his lunch of bread that tasted of something inorganic and cheese that had no taste at all. If he ate half now, half later, it would seem like more.

Well to the southeast, near the Connecticut River, he could see the ruined buildings of ex-Hartford. Just down the slope from him was abandoned land studded with private habitations that had been condemned long ago because of polluted water. Falling to pieces in the once-upon-a-time driveways of some of those houses were the cars their owners had left behind when they were evicted fifty or sixty years earlier. Even then there'd been no gasoline to move them anywhere. Ghost cars, everybody called them. Sitting beside ghost houses.

Where the land flattened out, about a mile from where he was resting, the zone of active housing began—first middle density, then the gray concrete blocks of the high density housing units, grouped around the factories and outlets and the administration buildings and barracks and official residences that made up Local Center 14.

Sirens began to moan down in the inhabited areas, then rose to a high whine and held it. An alert! Alerts could mean just about anything, from an outbreak of rats to a downward revision of safe solar exposure levels. Laddie thrust his arms through his shirt sleeves, buttoned cuffs and collar, set his cap squarely on his head, neck and ear guards down, and got going. Fast. Into the valley ahead.

The all-clear sounded just as he reached the middle density housing zone, but he stopped at a cluster of two-story habitations anyway, to get information.

He spotted a pair of bare feet resting on the parapet of the balcony of a second-floor apartment, parked his bike, and walked over to the entrance and read the name-plates, then backed off until he was underneath the feet. "Hey, Barbara," he called.

The feet pulled back in. A second later a young woman four or five years older than Laddie leaned over the parapet. Her bare shoulders suggested she was sunning naked. "Do I know you?" she asked.

"No, you don't. I got your name from the door," he replied. He wiped the sweat off his forehead with his shirttail, then smiled at her. "What were the sirens about? I was caught on the ridge when they tuned up."

"Just an announcement. There's going to be an oblig-atory statistics broadcast at six o'clock this evening. And—" Barbara hesitated, as if she didn't like to say the next thing—"and all heads of households with two de-pendent progeny are required to attend conferences with Council representatives late this afternoon."

"What's that all about? I come from a two-progeny household myself," Laddie said.

"I don't know," Barbara replied. "If you don't mind, I'll go back to my vitamin D." She lowered herself out of sight. Then up popped her head again and more shoulder than before. "You look pretty hot," she said. "Would you like some water?"

Laddie said he would, and wearing a bathrobe now, she brought down a glass. He told her his name and that he lived out in the valleys.

"I wish you *did* know me," he said, as he gave her back the glass.

"I'm not that type, Laddie."

She meant she wasn't coming on with him. She meant she wasn't one of the women who took on really young guys. Supposedly it happened a lot in the densely inhabited areas. Contraception rations weren't issued in NOR-SEC until one reached the age of twenty, and then only females got them. Younger girls and guys were supposed to "abstain" or face the consequences. But young guys could make out with rationed women all they wanted, because there'd be "no statistical effects" from it—the Council's way of saying "no babies."

Laddie got back on his bicycle. "Keep me in mind if you ever change your type, Barbara. Okay?"

"Okay. And good luck with this two-progeny thing. My older sister has two kids, too."

"I'll let you know if I find out anything about it in the Center. I come right by here on my way home."

□

About twenty people of all ages were lined up in front of the computer terminal at the personnel outlet. Laddie asked them about the recent announcement, but they didn't know any more about it than Barbara did. When it was his turn, Laddie inserted his disk in the slot and pushed INQUIRY. *Whirr-whirr.* Then a menu:

WHAT KIND OF INQUIRY
DO YOU WANT TO MAKE?

1) HEALTH

2) HOUSING

3) RATIONS

4) EMPLOYMENT

5) OTHER

Laddie punched 4.

More *whirr*s. Then, in that stupid way, the computer scrolled off information about him that he had to confirm before he could get on with his inquiry.

NAME: ARTHUR LADD GRAYSON;
      ANSWERS TO "LADDIE"

SEX: MALE

AGE: 17 YEARS, 5 MONTHS, 10 DAYS

HEIGHT: 5'11"; WEIGHT: 171 LBS.

HAIR: (COLOR) BROWN; (TEXTURE) CURLY

EYES: BLUE

BODY TYPE: MESOMORPH

AGILITY AND COORDINATION: EXCELLENT

ENERGY LEVEL (PHYSICAL): HIGH

STATUS: DEPENDENT PROGENY

RATIONS CLASSIFICATION: SUBADULT CLASS
A (MALE)

EDUCATION AND CHARACTER:

SCHOOLING: GENERAL TO AGE 15

TEST PLACEMENTS: MATH, UPPER 3%; VER-
BAL, UPPER 3%; MANIPULATIVE, UPPER 3%;
INGENUITIVE, UPPER 3%

ENERGY LEVEL (MENTAL): HIGH

MINDSET: LINEAR

CHARACTER: LOW PASSIVITY

BEHAVIOR RECORD: NO MARKS; 2 WARN-
INGS

SPECIAL COMMENTS: HAS NOT APPLIED TO
ATTEND COUNCIL SCHOOL ALTHOUGH
ELIGIBLE

EMPLOYMENT EXPERIENCE: NONE

WHEN YOU HAVE CHECKED THE ABOVE IN-
FORMATION (YOU ARE REMINDED OF THE SE-

VERE PENALTIES FOR ALLOWING PERSONAL
DATA TO BE MISREPRESENTED), PRESS ENTER
TWICE.

Laddie did so and got the familiar message.

THERE IS NO EMPLOYMENT FOR A SUBADULT
WITH YOUR QUALIFICATIONS.

Fed up, he decided to exhibit a little low-passivity behavior. He bicycled to the Records Office, where he ar-
gued his way past the guard by claiming his disk was
warped, and got to an elderly clerk. He said he'd been
trying for over two years to get a job, with no luck at all.
Was something wrong in his file? The clerk put down the
paper he was working on, took Laddie's disk, and went
away. A surprise. Usually the clerks refused to help at all,
though they were rationed just like the people who asked
them questions.

A few minutes later the clerk came back with an eras-
able printout of Laddie's data. "Is all the information
correct?" he asked.

Laddie looked at it—it was identical to what the computer at the personnel outlet had shown—and said it
was.

"Then nothing's wrong that *I* can see."

"Look, I'd be willing to take work I'm overqualified

for," Laddie said. "We need the extra ration points."

The clerk looked around over his glasses to make sure nobody was listening. "I notice you haven't applied for Council school," he whispered.

"Is *that* it?"

"It certainly doesn't help. Why haven't you applied?"

"Family reasons."

"They'd have to be pretty good ones to keep *me* from applying if *I* had the chance. You do well in the school and you can end up a Council member." The clerk smiled grimly. "Get so much food you throw it away. What *are* the reasons?"

"You have to live at home during your years in the Lower School, and that means your family has to live in the Center. Mom and Dad don't want to move. We live out in the valleys."

"Too bad—for you," the clerk said.

"That's the way I felt about it, as a matter of fact."

"It just may be a concealed mark against you."

"Would that mean that even after I turn eighteen, they won't find me a job?"

"Oh, they'll *find* you one." The clerk looked around again. "Cleanup and Repair, more than likely. Low ration points. High accident rate. One day you breathe in the wrong place at the wrong time and they take you away. Me, I'd go to the Council offices and apply for school right now, if I were you. Which isn't to say it may not be too late."

"I can't. I just can't," Laddie said.

"The Council doesn't believe in second chances. They don't believe in too many first ones."

Laddie ran his hand through his thick curly hair despairingly. "Sometimes I think, Why not run away?"

"*Shut up*, you young fool," the clerk hissed. "You could get us both in trouble. Anyway, there's no place to run away to." He went back to his papers. "No place where you won't fry or freeze or starve or rot. Or, sooner or later, tangle with smart rats."

"Yeah, I know. Say, have you heard anything about these two-progeny family conferences this afternoon?"

"Nothing at all, but it can't be good news. Tightest security I've about ever encountered. Move along now."

□

Although he would have liked to have something concrete to report to Barbara, Laddie didn't stop at the dry-goods distribution outlet where his father worked to find out if he'd been told any details about the conferences. Visitors weren't welcome, and anyway, it was unlikely Arthur Grayson would know anything if the clerk didn't. Laddie did go to the central edible-provisions outlet, however. His mother had given him the family rations disk so he could pick up some things she couldn't get at their local outlet. Laddie disked in, entered his requests, tossed the soap and synthoil that were handed him into the basket of his bike, and set off toward home.

Barbara was watering the plants by her front door. "You seem to spend all your time caring for the thirsty," Laddie said, as he came up behind her and touched her back. "I couldn't find out anything definite about the two-progeny business, except a clerk told me the security was really tight."

"That doesn't necessarily mean much."

"Maybe not, though I'd believe any bad news today."

"What makes today any worse than any other day?"

"I just got turned down—again—by the computer. No jobs for someone with my qualifications. And this morning my best friend, a guy named Sam Pratt, was deported. They put on this big ceremony; I—I'll never forget it." Tears welled up in Barbara's eyes as Laddie described the procedure. He said softly, "I cried this morning myself. I wouldn't admit it to anyone I know better, but I did."

"Good for you—for the crying. My lover—his name was Pete—Pete was deported last year. No ceremony like the one you describe. They just took him away."

"Trade and Barter?"

Barbara shook her head. She upended the pitcher of

water and shook the last drops out on a plant. "Pete was a specialist at welding tired metals. He refused to do some work on a bridge down near Long Island Sound if they wouldn't give him special clothing. He was found guilty of noncooperation. No appeal. He thought he was so specialized he'd be safe. He wasn't."

"Sam was really loyal. Brave, too. I think he'd have fought them today if they'd treated me the way they were treating him."

"They're too strong to fight," Barbara said. "I went through it. The worst of it is that they do such terrible things to people, and basically, they don't even care."

"The lieutenant cared. He was having a good time."

"We've got that over them."

"What do you mean?"

"Come back and tell me when you've figured it out."

"So I can come back?"

"Only to talk."

□

When Laddie got home, a little before four o'clock, he left his bike in the driveway and went inside. His mother was upstairs with Greta, Laddie's younger sister. She was the one who had done the terrible thing to Sam at the procedure that morning. It sounded as if an argument was going on—not unusual. Laddie called to let his mother know he was back from the Center with her groceries and was going out again. He asked if anything was up. She said, "Nothing in particular." That meant she didn't yet know about the conferences, which was understandable, because there were no sirens out where they lived to have alerted her to turn the radio on. If Laddie told his mother now, she'd want to talk about the conferences. Laddie had a meeting of his own to go to, so he left without saying anything more.

3

George Vibert was peering along the joints between the walls and the floorboards, and sniffing the air. "Are you sure this place is clean, Laddie?" he asked, when Laddie came in. George had to be extra careful. He had pale hair and very fair skin that irritated easily.

Laddie said, "You saw the procedure this morning, George. The contaminators didn't come near here."

They were in a small shed that had belonged to the Pratts. Situated a long way from the main house, hidden behind a rise and overgrown with sourbush, it was easily overlooked. Laddie and George Vibert and Joey Hernandez and Sam Pratt had used it as a clubhouse when they were still in school and had formed the club they'd called the Smart Rats, but they hadn't met formally in the last several years. Four boys, sixteen or seventeen years old, clubbing together, didn't really violate the regulations against assembly as they applied to rationed citizens. But you never knew how a magistrate might feel if someone reported it. The Council was careful.

When Joey Hernandez came in, Laddie revived one of the old rituals. He raised a hand and gave the club sign, two outer fingers raised, the other two gnawing at the thumb. He also said the password: "Ratpower."

"Come on," George said. "Act your age."

"It's in memory of Sam," Laddie said.

"Ratpower," Joey put in, and gave the sign just as Laddie had, except that Joey was left-handed. "I saw you signal Sam, Laddie. It took guts, with that lieutenant and his corpsmen there."

"I couldn't let Sam go off like that, as if nobody cared." Laddie hammered once on the wall, hard. His voice caught a little. "I really liked the guy."

"So did we," Joey said quietly.

"Think of the good times," George said. "Try to forget this morning."

"So many of them were good because of—of Sam," Laddie said, choking up.

"Hey!" Joey, who was big and powerful, the oldest-looking of the three, clenched a fist and flexed a biceps. "Smart Rats are tough."

"And they know their friends," Laddie said. "Sam never wore a stolen wristwatch."

George Vibert said, "His dad did confess. And in his job he had opportunities."

"My dad works at the same place Mr. Pratt did, don't forget," Laddie said. "Dad says he was the most honest supervisor they had. He got in someone's way. Or else they decided it was time to scare us."

"We don't know that," George said.

"Dad says if someone who works at a distribution outlet is condemned, they automatically condemn the rest of the family."

"Oh, come on, Laddie. They're not that arbitrary."

"Don't defend the system, George. Did you see Sam's welts?"

"Maybe he'd resisted," George said.

"Yeah, and maybe not," Laddie said.

"I don't like to think of what else might have happened to Emily," Joey said.

George said, "Why did you get us here, Laddie?" Laddie had gone to the other two boys after the contamination procedure to suggest that they meet that afternoon. "Come to the point. I don't like this conversation. And I've got to get home."

"I called a meeting so we could swear a solemn Smart Rats oath."

"That boring stuff again," George said.

"Swear we won't forget Sam. And that by God, if we ever get the chance, we'll revenge him."

"What kind of a crazy idea is that? Laddie, you're getting to be dangerous to know."

"And you're getting to be a pain in the ass, George," Laddie said.

"Easy, there, guys," Joey Hernandez said. "Say! We all belong to two-progeny households. You heard about the conferences?"

Laddie told them about how he'd been caught up on the ridge by the alert, when they announced the conferences, and about Barbara on the balcony. "This real nice tan on her shoulders. And down." He made a gesture.

"You think she might be available?" George asked, really interested for the first time in what Laddie was saying.

"She said she wasn't the type. But she said I could come back and see her."

"Tell her about your friends," George said. He went to the door. "I'm off now."

Laddie gave the secret sign to his back, glanced at Joey, and grinned. "Ratpower, guy," he called.

After George was out of earshot, Joey said, "I saw what Greta did this morning, Laddie."

"I can't stand to think about it, Joey. My own sister."

"She looks so—so kind of . . . innocent," Joey said. "What got into her?"

Laddie tapped his head. "She's not so innocent up there." He changed the subject. "How'd you like to have that lieutenant tied up and gagged and blindfolded? Right here in this shed. Right now."

"I wouldn't know what to do with him, Laddie."

"*I* would," Laddie said.

4

Nobody was in the kitchen, although there was food on the stove. Laddie went into the living room. "Hi, Mom. The hinge on the garage door is broken, by the way. It wasn't this morning. How did that happen?"

"Greta's had one of her days." Louise Grayson was in the stiff chair in front of the big window staring, in that fixed way she had, out toward the road. The profile view emphasized how sharp and nervous her face had become, although Laddie could remember when she was as pretty as Barbara on the balcony. "Where have you been, Laddie?"

"I called a meeting of our old club. Because of Sam."

"Be careful. People . . . report things. And everyone

knows what good friends you were with Sam."

"What are you looking at, Mom?" His mother hadn't once turned her head toward him.

"I'm looking in the direction of trouble."

"Look at *me*," Laddie said. It bothered him to have her look off while she talked to him, as if she were watching an enemy she could see but he couldn't.

Louise Grayson turned in the careful way she moved when her back was hurting. "Have you heard about the conferences, Laddie? For heads of two-progeny households?"

"Yeah. I heard about them at the Center."

"And you didn't tell me?"

"What was the point? I didn't know anything."

"Your father stopped by to change his clothes on his way to the meeting house. He told me then. Did you try for a job?"

Laddie nodded. "And got the usual turndown. A clerk told me it may be because I haven't applied to go to a Council school, although I'm eligible. That may be a concealed mark."

"I hope not." Louise Grayson sighed. "It's been a terrible day. I don't think I could get through many more like it. First the Pratts. I wasn't there, but I lived through it all the same. Then Greta broke the garage door just before you came back. Now this new thing. I'm so worried. It's so *late.* Your father's never been so late."

"And I'm really hungry," Laddie said.

"Turn on the radio. It's time for the six-o'clock obligatory statistics. Your father told me about that, too."

The announcer began with a routine report:

Pollution: A list of areas in NORSEC where leaks of buried chemicals were causing lung, eye, and alimentary alerts. New: in the inhabited inland belt of Long Island seven cases of blindness (thought to be only temporary) that resulted from exposure to sludge-tainted pelagic fogs. Not so new: a radioactivity alert was still in effect in the Hudson Valley from Kingston south as a result of leakage from the old Catskills nuclear-waste-storage facility.

Ozone: The continent-wide thinning had in some areas exceeded what was to be expected at this season. The situation was particularly bad in NORCENSEC, from the southern Great Lakes to Hudson Bay, where an ozone hole was expanding. The ozone situation continued acceptable over NORSEC.

Weather: A killing heat wave continued over the southern Rockies, fanning fires that had been burning for more than six weeks. A tropical storm in the Gulf of Mexico had broken through the dikes. Seawater had come as far inland as ex-Tallahassee. Three hundred thirty-one deaths were reported.

Vermin: Packs of so-called smart rats had launched an

invasion from the disinhabited area that bordered the Chesapeake Bay to the west and attacked food-storage facilities along the lower Susquehanna River. They had succeeded in occupying several granaries but were now being driven back by rodent attack teams. Three granary guards were reported dead of rat bite.

Then, at last, came the obligatory statistical report:

"The harvest estimates for the entire North American Jurisdiction have been completed by the College of Statisticians," the voice on the radio said. "Food supplies across the continent will be sharply below last spring's projections. Certain disinhabited areas recently put under reclamation have proved to be damaged beyond recovery; certain reclaimed areas will fall short of their anticipated contributions; and the estimates from traditionally productive inhabited areas are overall disappointing. The drought in NORWESEC, now in its eleventh year, has reduced harvest figures to twenty percent of those usual as recently as fifteen years ago. Stock animals in grazing regions are dying of thirst and starvation. Where there is still sufficient topsoil to support crops in NORCENSEC and SOUCENSEC, yields have been reduced by infestations of Destron-resistant insects, especially a new strain of summer thrips, and by rainbow rust. The NORSEC Statisticians advise that there will be a shortage of apples, because of the—"

Louise Grayson threw up her hands. "Apples? We live in NORSEC and we won't have *apples*? That's a first. We had all the apples we wanted, almost, just last fall. What'll they run out of next?"

"Statisticians, I hope," Laddie said.

"I wish they'd make *them* into sausage."

"It's bad enough already."

"If we come to cannibalism, and who's to say we won't, we might as well eat the worst first."

"What's for dinner?" Laddie said.

"Sausages," Louise replied.

Laddie had become aware of a figure lurking in the hall. "Why don't you come in here if you want to hear what we're saying? You eavesdrop so much, your ears are going to grow stalks."

"They're *not*!" Greta Grayson did come in, still wearing the blue shorts she'd had on that morning at the procedures and the light-blue shirt that set off her black hair and heavy, dark eyebrows. "Where's Daddy?" she said. "I'm hungry."

"He's not back yet and I love you and please don't make a scene *of any kind* right now," Louise Grayson said.

"I'm hungry, I'm hungry, I'm hungry, I'm hungry," Greta chanted.

Louise got up. As she limped toward the kitchen, Greta bumped her. Maybe it was an accident, but Laddie got ready to spring in case Greta tried more of her funny business. His mother seemed to him to be going slower than she would have just weeks before. Her back was worse and so was her hip, no doubt about it. They didn't dare ask for a diagnostic appointment. People who were taken to the Therapy Center too often didn't come back. But if she got much worse, someone would report her.

Louise unlocked the food cabinet and applied a smear of peanut butter to a cracker, which Greta gobbled down. Laddie watched from the living room door. His mother looked off somewhere else, in that way she had.

"Laddie, I gave it to her because she—because I can't bear it. To be hungry when you know why is one thing. But when you don't understand—"

"Greta understands plenty," he said.

"Don't hold it against her. Or . . . me," Louise Grayson pleaded.

"It's okay," he said.

"No it's not." There was static from the radio; the station was changing from the NORSEC announcer to something else. "Turn that thing off," Louise said. "I despise statistics. It is *not* okay."

"Look," he said, "I don't like to listen to Greta whine either. In fact, I don't like much of anything about Greta."

"We must love one another," Louise said, "hard though it may sometimes be."

A different announcer said, "We now bring you a message from the President of the Council of NORSEC."

"Wow!" Laddie made gagging sounds. "It's the boss."

☐

"As a result of the unfavorable statistical report you have just heard regarding the anticipated harvests in both this sector and in the other sectors of the North American Jurisdiction, the responsible Councils have determined that steps must be taken in order to deal in a timely way with the provisions shortfalls. Emergency programs will therefore be put into immediate effect in order to avoid the imposition of a continent-wide reduction of food rations.

"My fellow Council members, members of the conciliar colleges and corps and affiliated units, and rationed citizens, these are difficult times and they demand forceful and immediate action. Some of the new programs may seem harsh, but the alternative would be far worse. We will do what must be done, strong in our knowledge that it is right and necessary. Good evening."

☐

The original announcer came back on. Laddie killed the set.

His mother said, "I suppose one of the 'harsh new

programs' involves two-progeny households. I can't *bear* it."

Laddie said, "The rumor is they're going to cork us at both ends, so they can say we don't have any need for food."

"Where would they get enough cork?"

5

"Why the hell does Laddie have to leave that bike out here? Why can't he put it back in the garage where it belongs, the way I do mine?" The questions were shouted from the driveway. "He's broken the hinge on the door, too. What's the matter with that kid?"

"Your father's home. At last we'll have some news," Louise Grayson said.

Arthur Grayson came in the kitchen and glared at Laddie. "What did you do to the garage door?"

"I didn't do anything to it."

Louise said, "Forget the garage door. What was the conference about, Art?"

"That door worked perfectly well when I closed it this morning," Arthur said.

"That door worked perfectly well when *I* closed it this morning, too," Laddie said.

"It's broken now," his father said, as if he'd caught Laddie in a lie.

"It *is* broken now. You're right. But I didn't break it," Laddie said. "Greta did."

"There you go accusing her again."

"Rightly," Louise Grayson said. "She swung on it, though she's been told often enough not to. Art, please. What—"

Arthur looked around, like someone afraid of an ambush. "Where is Greta?" he asked.

"I don't know. She was just here. Won't you *please* tell us what the conference was about, Art?"

"Can't you give a man a few seconds of peace so he can say hello to his children?" Arthur clapped Laddie on the shoulder. The carping was over for the time being. "D'you have a good day?"

"What a question!—considering how it began."

"I've been going crazy, sitting here waiting for you, Art," Louise said. She limped over to the stove and turned the knobs, as if she'd have liked to wrench them off the control panel. "This stuff might as well be warming up," she said. "Now won't you please *tell* us?"

Her husband's lips tightened. He looked at the floor.

Greta came back into the room, dancing a little so everybody had to notice her.

"Hi there, honey," Arthur said. "Come get a kiss. Good to see you."

"Laddie said when he brought me back home this morning, he'd be glad if he *never* had to see me again."

"Tell her you didn't mean it," Louise Grayson said.

"Tell me, tell me, tell me, tell me, tell me," Greta chanted.

"I did mean it," Laddie said. "And she knows why, too. If there was any justice, her foot would fall off."

"What does *that* mean? What's the matter with you, Laddie? Why do you say things like that?" Arthur Grayson said angrily. "No wonder she's so high-strung."

"She tripped Sam as he went by her this morning. That's why he fell." Laddie described to his mother what had happened.

"She did *not* do any such thing," Arthur said.

"Oh yes she did, Dad. You were too scared to notice."

"Did you, honey?" Greta shook her head. "There."

"Maybe you should believe me, not her," Laddie said. "Sometimes I get sick and tired of it."

"If she did trip Sam, I'm sure it was a mistake," Louise said.

"Laddie hit me, too, Daddy," Greta put in. "He hit me right here." She pointed to a place on her ankle.

"You did *that* swinging on the garage door," Laddie guessed, "but next time you do anything like what you did this morning, I will hit you."

"Don't threaten her, Laddie," Arthur Grayson said. "It's hard enough on your mother and me as it is."

"The conference, Art. Tell us *now*, Art. You *have* to."

Arthur closed his eyes, about to begin, but Greta interrupted him. "Be a chair," she said.

"Not tonight, Greta, honey."

"Be a *chair*," she screamed. "A *chair*, a *chair*, a *chair*, a *chair*, a *chair*—"

Louise said, hopelessly, "Go ahead. She won't give us any peace otherwise."

Arthur squatted down. He put his back flat against the outside door and positioned his feet and lower legs so his upper thighs were horizontal. Greta went to him, turned around, sat on his knees, and began to bounce.

"Now, Art. *Now!*" Louise said.

"They called us in to tell us about a new program." Arthur lost his balance and had to brace himself with stiffened fingers. "That's enough, honey. You're pretty heavy." He eased Greta off his knees and stood up. "A progeny reduction and relocation program," he said slowly. "They've decided to reduce the progeny limit to one instead of two per household. Nobody can have more than one from now on, Louise."

"What's that got to do with *us*? We had our kids when

two was the limit. We had them under the old system, Art."

"Families that have two progeny already are going to be . . . reduced. They're going to be cut back to one."

"How can they do that? Two's two! *Two* is *two*!"

"The Council is going to take charge of one progeny from each household."

"Take charge? What does *that* mean?"

"Take them away so there'll be only one left. So all households will have just one progeny."

"I don't get it, Art."

"I can't say it any clearer, Louise."

"Take them *where*?" she cried.

"I don't know. They'll become wards of the Council. Councils, actually. The program's continent wide. Maybe worldwide. They're sending them to some newly reclaimed areas below the Equator, that's all they're telling us.

"When?"

"Soon. I don't know just when."

"For how long?" Louise screamed.

Arthur Grayson's voice dropped to a bare whisper. "Forever." He took his wife in his arms. "One of our kids is going away forever, Louise."

"Which one will they take?"

"That's up to the Council. They're sending magistrates who'll decide. It'll be their choice."

Louise fainted. Arthur said, "Oh, my God. Oh, my God," and lowered her gently to the floor. "Oh, my God."

"Is she dead?" Greta asked.

Arthur said, "Laddie, the stove."

Laddie wheeled and turned down the heat. Supper was burning, and they hadn't even noticed.

MAGISTRATE'S CHOICE

6

"I shouldn't have told her," Arthur Grayson whispered, as he and Laddie carried Louise to the couch in the living room. He knelt beside her.

"What are you talking about, Dad? You had to tell her. And me. And Greta, too."

"Maybe you," Arthur said. "You're almost a grown man."

"Isn't Mom a grown woman? And Greta's . . . in on it."

"She's too young to understand."

"Do you think she understood what was happening this morning?"

"I think this is no time to go into *that* again." Arthur

rubbed Louise's hands. "Forgive me," he whispered. "Please forgive me."

"Dad, that's just . . . not the point," Laddie said. He tried to get his father on track. "What more do you know about this new program, Dad? It sounds really terrible."

"And having your mother faint isn't? I have to deal with what's right in front of me before I can deal with things that are farther away."

Greta, who'd followed them to the living room, went back to the kitchen. "I'm hungry, I'm hungry, I'm hungry," she began.

Arthur said, "You'll have to wait until your mother's recovered, honey."

"I don't want to wait. I'm hungry."

"We're all hungry, but we all have to wait, honey."

"If you don't come in here and give me something to eat *right now*," Greta said, "I'm going to tell people you're stealing things and trading them, just like Mr. Pratt."

"*Now* what do you think?" Laddie said. "About Greta and this morning."

"I think I'd better go speak to her." Arthur went to the kitchen and placed his hands on Greta's shoulders. He bent over and kissed her forehead and said, "Honey, you mustn't ever, not *ever*, say that again or I won't be a chair for you."

Greta said, "Yes you will."

Louise Grayson tried to sit up. "What happened? Oh—I remember. My God. Oh, my God." She moved her hands nervously over her face and hair. "What are the details, Art? Tell me the rest."

"It'll keep. Enough is enough," he said.

"I'm not going to faint again," she said.

"Later," he said firmly, "when we've all had a chance to collect ourselves. We *should* eat now. Greta thinks so and she's right. It won't make it all any better if we go hungry. It's not the end of the world, anyway. We'll manage to get through this one the way we have everything else. Put supper on the table, Laddie. I'll stay with your mother."

"I can't eat," Louise said, "but you should. Go ahead, Laddie."

"Keep Greta with you, Dad," Laddie said. "Otherwise she might steal an extra hunk of scorched statistician so she can trade it for an electric prod."

"I just don't understand how you can joke at a time like this," Arthur Grayson said.

☐

Laddie took Greta for her walk that evening as he did every evening. His father was usually too tired to take her, and so much walking wasn't good for Louise Grayson. The walks seemed to flush out Greta's brain. Without them she couldn't sleep in a good way anymore. Greta had had good sleep and bad sleep the last year or two. She thrashed and whimpered and sweated when she was having bad sleep, and someone had to go to her and deal with the way she acted when she was awakened in the middle of the night.

They were hardly down the driveway and on Bentham Road before Greta began to play her game. Laddie could tell from the way she hip-hopped back and forth across the blacktop ahead of him. The rule was that she had to step or hop or jump from one break to another in the pavement, as fast as she could, and never put both feet on the ground at once or put a foot on a solid patch of blacktop. The game wasn't all that hard to play, because of the condition of the road.

Meanwhile Laddie was worrying. There was a real crisis in the making with this progeny program. Crisis was the rule of life in NORSEC, but this one was exceptional. The Ultimate Crisis. Capital U, capital C.

He didn't want to be chosen and have to leave home. Say good-bye to everybody—forever. Just thinking about it made him homesick.

And he didn't want to fall into the hands of the Council. He hadn't needed the morning's procedures to know you couldn't trust them.

The other possibility wasn't much better. Though she did terrible things, Greta was his sister, and he remembered her when she was okay. Even fun. Easier to love than now. Suppose the Council magistrate chose her. What would become of her when she wouldn't have Laddie to take her for walks, Louise for a constant baby-sitter, and their father for a chair?

Greta lost her balance and had to put both feet down at once, but she went right on. She was cheating at her own game.

Maybe, if she got chosen to go, she'd learn to get along on her own. Maybe it would be good for her.

Maybe not.

And maybe, if Laddie had a mark against him for not applying for school, and was going to get a high-risk job, he'd actually be better off in the new program.

And maybe not. Squared.

Above all, Laddie didn't want to say good-bye to everybody. That was the way he thought about it: saying good-bye. The idea made his stomach turn over.

To get his mind off the new program, he decided to take Greta on.

They were almost at the turn into Malthus Drive, where Joey Hernandez lived. Laddie began to overtake Greta, going from one break to another, following her rules, back and forth across the road. She saw that he was getting nearer, hopping the way she was, only a lot faster, and realized what he was doing. She tried to speed up and escape him.

"That's at least three errors," he yelled when she made a bunch of mistakes. "That's going to cost you."

He was enjoying himself, but Greta wasn't taking it as a game. She had her wild look. Good. She needed to be hammered on for what she'd done that morning. Laddie pulled to the left, got in front of her, turned her, and forced her up into Malthus Drive, where she didn't want to go. She didn't like it when Joey or his sister Flor joined in on one of their walks in the evening, and to get them was usually the reason Laddie took her up Malthus.

He herded Greta now, staying a few feet from her but never giving her any chance to break away. When they reached the Hernandez house, he feinted to the left but jumped to the right, and touched her with both index fingers, on the throat. "*Ping-ping!* Double dead."

She crouched and faced him, like the rats on the Council posters.

He said, "I own you now."

"You do not."

"Yes, I do." He pretended to write something on his left palm.

"What are you writing?"

"Your score, and all about how you were cheating, too. And that you're in my power. And that maybe I'll have you personally contaminated and deported because of the way you act. Unless you agree to be obedient."

"For how long?"

"An hour. I'm going to get Joey and Flor and we're going to walk, and you're going to walk a hundred feet ahead of us. Walk quietly, as if you were going with Dad to religious meeting on Sunday. Got it?" Greta nodded. "Stay right here. Don't move and don't make a noise. Got that?"

He didn't wait for an answer or look back as he strutted up to the Hernandez house, imitating Lieutenant Lindgren.

Joey answered the door. "How about a walk?" Laddie said. "Bring Flor, too."

"No way. They're all sitting in there staring at each other. I can't leave."

"What are Smart Rats saying about this new program?" Laddie gave the sign.

Joey responded with just his left middle finger. "Did you catch the local seven-o'clock news?" he asked. "No? Then you missed the latest."

Greta had started up toward them; Laddie's power wasn't enough to keep her out in the street for very long. How and when she learned more about this program was up to their father, so Laddie told Joey to wait a minute and went down to her.

"Do you think you can find the back way to the pond?" The "back way" was what they called a little side trail that went in from Malthus and joined the main Bentham Pond trail. Greta nodded. "You go on ahead, then. I'll meet you there in a little while, Greta." She was smiling now, her dark eyes glittering with excitement. To go to the pond was one of the big things in her life, and going there by herself for the first time ever had to be about the biggest. "And if you ever tell Mom or Dad I let you go to the pond alone, you'll lose your right eye. You understand?" Greta nodded some more and hip-hopped off.

Joey and Laddie stood next to the Hernandez's old rural delivery mailbox as they talked. "What just came over the radio is the schedule for our Center," Joey said. He twisted the mailbox, which hung facedown by a single nail, so it balanced upright. "The Council magistrate is going to have his meeting with parents and progeny from our mile on Wednesday afternoon." The mailbox sank slowly back. "Random pickups will begin next Monday."

"What does *that* mean?" Laddie asked.

"Didn't your dad tell you about the pickups?"

"He didn't tell us much, as a matter of fact. Mom got pretty upset, so he put it off until later."

"They call it a 'Random Pickup Procedure.' Do you realize there are only five households with two dependent progeny in this entire mile? And we're actually four miles hooked together under one master."

"Noted," Laddie said. "Get back to the pickup business."

"The random part means that they'll take us away according to random selection, done by computer. Nobody from the same mile goes in the same bus, that idea. So we won't know anybody. Won't have any friends. Be really separated from everybody, not just family. And if you're chosen to go on Wednesday, you may be picked up as early as next Monday."

"That's not a lot of time to say . . . good-bye."

"And not only will you not know where you're going before you leave, but your family won't know after you're there."

"Oh, come on. What about letters? And visits?"

"Short letters will be allowed, but only at long intervals. And no place names or anything like that. They say there's just not going to *be* any real ongoing communication between the kids taken away and their families. The brochure of the program says it's so everybody will realize the break is complete and permanent."

"What brochure?"

"The one they handed out. Your dad must have a copy. So anyway, they don't want a lot of inquiries and applications and petitions and complaints. People trying to get their kids back. Kids trying to return. Everybody unhappy and unsettled."

"Have they said what they'll base their choices on?" Laddie asked.

Joey shook his head. "It wasn't on the radio, and they

didn't tell it to my dad and yours this afternoon, either, and it's not in the brochure. A magistrate will meet with the families involved and make his decision, and that will be that." Joey twisted the mailbox again. This time the nail broke and the box fell to the ground. "I suppose there'll be different reasons, depending on the individual case. But the basic idea is to cut back on the population and the drain on food supplies, right? Plus reopen some disinhabited areas. Dad thinks they'll take the kids who eat the most. If so, Laddie, you and I, we'll be the ones to go, since Flor and Greta are younger. George, too." Joey shrugged hopelessly. "I don't know how much it matters," he said. "Here or south of the Equator, they've still got us by the balls."

Laddie tried to sound tougher than he felt. "Remember Ratpower, guy."

"Ratpower didn't help Sam much this morning."

☐

Sourbush grew just about everywhere in that part of NORSEC, but it was rankest where there was plenty of water, even when the water was polluted. A person who didn't know the path along the stream to Bentham Pond pretty well would have thought in the twilight that there wasn't a path at all. Even Laddie got confused a couple of times that evening and found himself clawing his way to nowhere, partly because, worried about Greta, he was in too big a hurry.

Trees grew near the pond, grew there naturally, not specially planted and treated like those around the administration buildings at the local center. They weren't all that stunted either. In fact, they put out enough shade in some places to stunt the sourbush. Yellow glo-cards had been nailed to each of their trunks.

THIS TREE IS PROTECTED BY ORDER
OF THE COUNCIL—DO NOT TOUCH

The cards gleamed in the light of the rising moon as Laddie approached the water. The Council's eyes never shut.

Greta and he always stopped on the bank of the pond near where the stream flowed into it, the shallow side where there was sand and a lot of pebbles. She liked to toss pebbles into the water, and she'd have liked to go wading, but Laddie couldn't let her because it got deep very quickly; also they didn't analyze the water for toxic chemicals anymore. Tonight she wasn't there.

He looked around and found her in the worst possible place—out on the concrete dam where she was never supposed to go. She was sitting down, her legs dangling over its slippery side as if she were about to ease herself off.

Midway across the dam was a narrow spillway. There'd been rain recently. A lot of water was going over, making plenty of noise. Possibly Greta wouldn't hear if he called to her, but in any case it was risky for her to come back on the narrow walkway by herself. She didn't know how to swim and neither did Laddie (it was illegal for rationed citizens to learn to swim, since rivers were a natural barrier for runaways), so he couldn't go in after her if she fell, and the water at the center of the dam was at least eight feet deep.

Laddie walked slowly around the shore, really scared. Greta saw him just as he reached the place where the path joined the approach to the dam. He waved. She didn't move. If he stayed where he was, she might fall in, either now or when she tried to leave. If he went after her, she might run from him and fall. But he had to do something.

He began to make flying motions. He waved his arms and veered left and right, made a few twirls, then soared toward the dam, arms out, flapped some more, stepped up on it, and pretended to glide until he was as near to her as he dared go.

She tensed up, but she was curious. "Why are you waving your arms?"

"Obviously I'm flying."

"I could *swim* if *I* wanted to," she said.

"Don't try it."

"I could. Someday I *will.*"

"Speaking of swimming, look at the slimy." Laddie pointed to her right. Nothing much lived in that water, but Greta didn't believe it and was always looking for what she called "slimies." When she craned in the direction he'd pointed, Laddie moved in on her, grabbed her neck and arm, and jerked her back from the edge.

She struggled. He was a lot stronger than she was, but she was resourceful. First she tried to pull him toward the water side, then she pulled toward the downspill side, where they'd have fallen on boulders. When that failed, she gave up suddenly to make him lose his balance. He had to let go of her, so if he fell she wouldn't go with him. As he was teetering, she shoved at his legs. He almost went over into the deep water, but he stepped back out of her reach, got his balance, grabbed her again, and dragged her to safety.

When they were on the bank, he squatted so his face was at the same level as hers. "Look at me. Mom and Dad think you don't understand things. I think you do. Do you realize what you just did?" Her glare reminded him of rat posters again. "You just tried to drown me, didn't you?"

"I don't care whether you drown or not," she said.

"I know that, now. I didn't before." He stood up. "I guess I'll have to treat you differently from now on."

"I don't care about that, either."

Laddie decided not to tell his parents what had happened. They'd have a fit because he'd let Greta go to the pond alone and, if he told them what she'd tried to do, wouldn't believe him.

Bad signals were flashing. Greta had been a problem for some years—willful and strange. A year earlier and she might have screamed and even struggled there on the dam, nothing more. Now she was dangerous. Like their mother, she seemed to be getting worse. Whatever was wrong with *her* was progressing, too.

□

When Laddie got Greta back to the house, it was almost dark. Only a small light burned in the downstairs hall. He let go of her hand so she could run to her room, then checked the living room to make sure his parents weren't sitting in the dark, as they sometimes did to avoid using up ration points. No. They'd gone to bed, but he had business with them too important to wait until tomorrow. He knocked on their bedroom door.

Arthur called to come in. He turned on a lamp.

"You feeling better, Mom?" Laddie asked.

"I'm going to live," Louise said, "although I don't know if I really want to."

"Of course she does," Arthur Grayson said soothingly.

Laddie said, "Dad, Joey tells me you were given a brochure about the progeny program. With details and so on."

"There's nothing—nothing much in it."

"I can't *believe* you didn't show it to me earlier."

"It's only four pages long."

"I want to see it," Laddie said. "Right now."

"Don't give me orders in that tone of voice."

"Dad. *Please*, Dad. My whole life's at stake."

"And don't be so thoughtless. Saying things like that is only going to upset your mother even more."

"Dad, *where is it?*"

"In my top dresser drawer."

Laddie got the brochure and brought it near to the lamp. There wasn't too much in it he didn't already know, but he found a statement about exceptions. There wouldn't be any, and application for them shouldn't be made. The statement had an asterisk beside it, however, and at the end he found a footnote.

"Did you read the small print?" he asked slowly. "Page four?"

"Why, no, I didn't."

"I'll read it aloud to you."

"Laddie, don't. I can't stand any more of this," Louise said.

Laddie ignored her. " 'The following exceptions are authorized. a) If one of the two progeny in a given domestic unit is within fifteen days of becoming eighteen as of the date this program is announced, that unit will be considered as having only a single dependent progeny and the program will not apply. b) If an unchosen progeny dies before the chosen progeny is picked up and taken away, the chosen progeny will be allowed to remain in place of the unchosen one and that domestic unit will be considered to have only a single dependent progeny.' "

"We don't fit," Arthur Grayson said.

"How about this? 'c) When one progeny in a two-progeny unit is in a Council school, that unit shall be considered exempt from this program, inasmuch as one progeny is already the ward of the Council.' "

Neither Arthur nor Louise said anything.

"Is that why you didn't show me this brochure? So I wouldn't read that?"

"I told you I hadn't read the small print."

"I don't believe you."

"Leave your father alone, Laddie."

"If you had let me apply, this wouldn't be happening," Laddie said bitterly.

Louise said, "You *know* the reasons, Laddie. Why harp on it?"

"I know you limp a little and Greta's not exactly normal—"

"Be quiet. She'll hear you," Arthur said.

"And for that, not only has my chance to go to a Council school been spoiled, but also I'll probably never get a decent job. And now one of us, Greta or me, is going to be taken away. Forever."

"There have to be priorities in any family, Laddie," Louise said, beginning to cry.

"Is that what I'm supposed to tell myself if I'm chosen?"

"Laddie, your mother's right. We're not alone in this world. Sometimes we have to make sacrifices for those we love."

Laddie tossed the brochure back into his father's dresser drawer. "You know, all that's just fine, except it only seems to work one way. Sometimes I think I don't matter very much around here."

"Laddie, your mother *fainted* tonight. Can't you be decent?"

"I try, but it's getting to be harder and harder."

"Then you must try harder," Louise whispered.

☐

A courier came to the Graysons' house the next day from Local Center 14 and delivered an envelope, which Laddie gave to his father when he got home. He waited while his father opened it.

Arthur groaned. "Why does it have to be *my* turn to

be milemaster when all this is happening? Why couldn't it have rotated to another head of household? It's not as if I get much in return for what I do. A few ration points. And I stand out, which can lead to trouble." Arthur waved the paper. "We have to be ready to go to the Center at noon tomorrow. They're sending a bus around. I've got to meet it over at the bus stop so I can direct the driver where to go. And now, tired as I am, I've got to get back on my bike and notify everybody."

Laddie did it for him, though it probably wasn't legal. The trade-off was that Arthur had to take Greta for her walk after dinner.

7

The five families from Mile 7 were collected in an old school bus, which thumped and coughed around the potholes and wash-outs in the road to the Center. They rumbled past Barbara's place (Laddie looked for feet on her balcony as they went by, but none showed) and past the pencil factory and the battery factory and some lesser administrative buildings, then stopped at a gate in the fence that separated the main Council buildings from the rest of the Center. The driver showed a paper to an Enforcement Corps corporal, then proceeded to Building J, where a messenger checked names, then led the group inside and sat everyone on hard wooden benches in a waiting room outside one of the judgment chambers.

The four windows, set high up in the walls, and the enforcement corpsmen, fully armed, stationed in antiriot cages, gave the waiting room the feeling of a prison.

At one o'clock the inner door opened and a lieutenant in the uniform of the Elite Female Cadre of the corps came out, followed by four ordinary corpsmen—three male, one female—who walked in formation behind her.

She approached the group from Mile 7. "Arthur and Louise Grayson and their progeny, Arthur and Greta, rise and follow me." To the other families she said, "Remain where you are and do not talk to each other."

She led the Graysons into the judgment chamber, a somewhat brighter room that had a low platform at one end on which sat a heavy desk and a small table. In front of the desk, on the floor level, sat four wooden chairs. The magistrate, in blue robes, was already at the desk. In front of him were papers and, to one side, turned toward him, a computer monitor. The clerk who was seated at the table also had a monitor, and a keyboard as well.

The lieutenant approached the magistrate and saluted. "Sir, present before you is the first domestic unit from Mile Seven. Name, Grayson."

"Seat them, seat them."

The lieutenant brought the Graysons to the wooden chairs. Laddie sat to the far right, while his mother and father flanked Greta . . . just in case.

The magistrate read the top paper in his pile, then looked over at the Graysons, his heavy-lidded eyes expressing little interest. He motioned the lieutenant to his side, whispered something, and the lieutenant gave a low order to her corpsmen, who had been standing back. They came forward and stood directly behind the Graysons, a corpsman to each member of the family. The magistrate then turned to his clerk and nodded.

The clerk stood and began to read. "In accordance with the procedure established by the Subcommittee on Population, acting in conjunction with the Subcommittee for Law and Order, of the governing Council of NORSEC, I will now read the operative sections of the decree in which the Progeny Reduction and Relocation Program is promulgated.

" 'It has been determined that there will be established a program for the purpose of reducing the progeny in the area governed by the Council, which will be achieved by two means.

" 'The first is that no domestic unit may hereafter have more than one progeny.

" 'The second is that those domestic units that have already produced two progeny, under the former population control guidelines, will have their progeny reduced to one, in the following manner. . . .' "

He read on for several minutes. When he was finished, he said to the Graysons, "You have heard the decree. Do you understand it? If so, please signify by raising your right hands." The clerk turned to the magistrate. "Sir—" he began, but stopped. The magistrate had fallen asleep. His head was tipped forward, his chin was resting on the ruffle at his collar, and his blue-and-white cap had loosened and fallen over his right eye. Wisps of gray hair were sticking out from under it. *"Sir,"* the clerk said more urgently.

"Eh? What is it? Proceed," the magistrate said testily. He looked at the clerk, then at the lieutenant, finally at the Graysons, his eyelids slowly lowering again.

The clerk stepped over, murmured to him, and straightened the cap, then said, in a louder voice, "The domestic unit present before you for the choice procedure has been read the decree and has acknowledged understanding of it."

"Bring up their data," the magistrate said, coming fully awake. After the clerk had keyboarded a command into the computer, the magistrate read from his own monitor. "Grayson," he said. "Milemaster. Mmm. Is that correct, Clerk?" The clerk said it was. "Good. The computer's working. Now . . ." The magistrate turned to the Graysons. "I will presently be invoking the guidance program set up to assist me in making my choices. Before I do so, each of you has the right to stand in turn and signify whether or not he or she has anything to say." He nodded to Arthur. "You go first."

Arthur stood up. "Sir," he said, "as you can see from the records, our son is within a few months of his majority, and—"

"Irrelevant," the magistrate said with a wave of his hand. "That's a point we'll be hearing over and over again," he remarked to the clerk.

Arthur persisted. "And it seems only fair that—"

"Irrelevant, I told you," the magistrate said. "The terms of the decree specifically state that only a progeny who'll be of age within fifteen days of the date of the promulgation of the decree will be exempt from the program. If you have nothing further to say, please sit down."

Arthur sat down.

Louise stood. "I want to object to the whole decree," she said, her voice rising. "It isn't fair. We had our progeny legally. It isn't fair for you to take one of them away after telling us it was all right to have them in the first place. It isn't fair."

"That is the law," the magistrate said.

"But now, after so many years, to lose one of our—"

"That is the law and there's nothing to be done about it and nothing to be gained from complaining," the magistrate said. "You, young Arthur Grayson. Do you want to say anything?" Laddie stood and shook his head. "Greta Grayson, have you anything to say?"

"No," Arthur said.

"I didn't ask you," the magistrate said. "Greta, have you anything to say?" Greta, who'd been told over and over not to speak under any circumstances, sat still. "I must have some kind of response from you to enter into the record of this hearing, Greta, as you are ten years of age. Shake your head if you have nothing to say."

"Go ahead, honey," Arthur said.

Greta shook her head.

"Well. At last we can get to the choice," the magistrate said. The clerk keyboarded something else while the magistrate watched his monitor. "Hmm," he said. He looked over at the Graysons, then back at his monitor, then at the clerk, who was reading the message on his own monitor. "Really," the magistrate said. "What a bore. The very first hearing and it balks. Try it again."

The clerk did so.

"Hmm. Same thing. Well—" The magistrate again turned to the Graysons. "The advisory program is inconclusive in your case. There are pros and cons regarding each progeny." He rubbed his eyes and tipped his head back. "You, young Arthur Grayson, would you care to explain why you didn't apply to attend a Council school?"

Laddie said, "Sir, at the time I—"

"Stand up when you address the magistrate," the clerk said.

Laddie stood. "Well, sir, at the time I wasn't sure that was what I wanted to do."

"Didn't anyone explain to you what a privilege it is?"

"I guess I didn't listen."

The magistrate turned to the lieutenant. "Isn't *that* typical? And they complain that we overgovern! He ends up marked as potentially noncooperative, and it was probably only stupidity and laziness. Bring the extended advisory program up on the screen."

He read his monitor. "Hmmm. Still the choice isn't very clear. I am at liberty, when the choice is not clear in the computer, to consult the parents of the progeny. Have *you* any preference in this matter?"

"What do you mean?" Louise said.

"Stand up, Mrs. Grayson," the clerk said.

"Oh, let her sit if she wants to," the magistrate said crossly. "I mean that if you will tell me which of your progeny you would prefer to go into the program, I am at liberty to be guided by your request."

"You expect us to do that?" Louise tangled her fingers in her hair. "You really expect us to do *that*?"

"Don't raise your voice to the magistrate," the clerk said.

"There might be many reasons, Mrs. Grayson, why you'd have a preference," the magistrate said, getting more irritated. "That's all I'm saying. Do you care which of them goes?"

"*Care?* Of course I *care*," Louise said. "I'll make the choice. I choose neither. *Neither!*"

"Disallowed. Mr. Grayson, could you try to be more reasonable than your wife? Have *you* a preference?"

Arthur said, "I'd have to consult with her."

"We'll be here all afternoon," the magistrate said. "Look, I'm offering you a privilege. I'm not imposing a choice on you, I'm allowing you to make it. I fancy you're almost bound to have some slight preference. Express it. Take advantage of your opportunity."

Louise jumped up. "You call it a *privilege?*" she screamed. "To let us decide which child to lose, you call that an opportunity? You with your fine clothes and your guards and—"

"Mrs. Grayson," the clerk said, shocked. "Remember where you are and to whom you are speaking."

"I'm not likely to forget it." Louise addressed the magistrate again. "Your robes and your guards and *your* privileges and your heartlessness. You tell us to decide which of our children we'll never see again and you can't even stay awake, you're so *bored* by what's going on. Don't you have kids of your own? I hope if you do one of them dies. Tonight."

Louise started toward the desk. The female corpsman who'd been stationed behind her moved forward and locked her arms so roughly Louise cried out, then dragged her back and pushed her down into her chair.

The magistrate's expression didn't change, but there was a change in his voice. He was no longer bored. He said, "I am formally invoking one of the alternative modes of choice. The choice of which of your progeny will be chosen for the relocation program *must* be made by you, Mr. and Mrs. Grayson."

"No," Louise cried. "Oh, please no."

"I have spoken formally from the chair. Make your choice."

"Mercy," she moaned. "Mercy."

"That is what I am showing you. Choose."

"Please, sir," Arthur said.

"Choose," the magistrate said, in a louder voice.

Louise was crying now. Arthur lifted Greta from her seat, put her in his own, then sat down next to his wife and held her.

"Choose," the magistrate said, "or by heavens I'll send both of them away. Choose, I say. *Choose!*"

Greta jumped up and danced around. "Choose, choose, choose, choose, choose," she chanted.

The corpsman assigned to her glanced at the lieutenant, who signaled to let the dance continue. The clerk and the lieutenant and all the guards were smiling now. Even the magistrate's mouth twitched slightly.

Arthur whispered to Louise. She moaned. He whispered again and clutched her arm. She whispered back. He turned to the magistrate and said something.

"I can't hear you."

"We choose our—our son to go into the program," Arthur said.

The magistrate nodded. "So be it," he said. "Clerk, enter the name of their son and request a random pickup date."

The clerk keyboarded, and a moment later the magistrate said, "Arthur Ladd Grayson, progeny of Arthur Grayson and Louise Ladd, of Mile Seven, Local Center Fourteen, of the Northeast Sector of the North American Jurisdiction, will be picked up for participation in the Progeny Relocation Program on Wednesday, October Twenty-sixth." He looked at Laddie. "You will be sent all necessary information about your random pickup and your subsequent participation in the relocation program. Take them away, Lieutenant."

The lieutenant led the Graysons back to the waiting room and seated them opposite the other families from Mile 7. She then crossed the room.

"Raoul and Maria Hernandez and their progeny, José and Flor, stand up and follow me."

Louise said, "Say something to Laddie, Arthur."

"Why don't you say something?"

"I can't." Tears were streaming down her face. "I can't say anything to him. You have to. *Say* something, Art. Say something to make it all right."

Laddie was sitting stiffly, his hands on his knees. Arthur grabbed his right hand but Laddie pulled it back. Arthur tried to take it again. Laddie knocked his father's hand away.

"*Say* something, Art."

Arthur rubbed his fingers. "You can never do everything for everybody, Laddie, no matter how much you'd like to. Don't think what just happened was easy." Suddenly, he, too, began to cry. Once again he reached out to Laddie.

"Stop, Dad. I don't want anyone to—to handle me."

"You're a fine boy. You know we think you are, Laddie."

Laddie edged down the bench to get away from his father.

"Greta's so . . . young and so— You're strong." Arthur worked closer to Laddie and once again reached toward him. "The strong can take care of themselves. But other people have to take care of the weak."

"Sure, Dad. Sure." Laddie moved some more.

A corpsman came over. "Quiet here. You're forbidden to talk."

Arthur didn't pay any attention. "You've got to understand, Laddie, that we only did it—"

"I *do*. I *do*. Pull yourself together, Dad."

"*Silence!*"

"I'd go in your place if they'd have me, Laddie," Arthur whispered.

"It's okay. It really is okay. I understand, Dad."

"Silence, I say. And close in."

There was a commotion at the doorway. Another bus had arrived, bringing families from another mile for their hearing. The guard went down to the end of the room.

"You really do understand, Laddie?"

"Yes, I really do. I don't mind going all that much. It'll be an opportunity, Dad."

"I believe you, Laddie. You hear that, Louise? He understands. He doesn't mind going. I do believe you, Laddie. You've got so much get-up-and-go that I believe you. I had it, too, when I was your age. You're a good son." Arthur took hold of Laddie's arm.

"Please don't, Dad."

"You make me feel a lot better, Laddie."

Laddie turned his head away.

CONTAMINATION

8

Laddie checked with Joey and George as they were all being taken home. They, too, had been chosen. In both their cases it had been routine, based on their being older than their sisters. George would be going the following Monday, the first possible pickup day. Joey would go three weeks later, on October 5th. Laddie didn't tell them how he had come to be chosen. He let them think it was because he, too, was older, as if his parents had done something he should be ashamed of.

For the next few days he kept to himself. Each morning he packed some lunch, took the bicycle, and went to miles he'd never been to before. He rode and rode and rode until he was so tired he had to stop; then after a rest he'd ride again. He rode upriver all the way to the boundary of the Oxbow disinhabited area. Went downriver to the edge of the sanitary zone that bordered Long Island Sound, beyond which the miasmas made it unsafe to travel. The wind was drifting out of the south that day, and he could smell the pollution and feel it on his skin and in his eyes before he turned around.

On Saturday he took a double ration of food, enough for both lunch and dinner, and went east to the Berkshires, which took him through a checkpoint into the jurisdiction of Local Center 12. There was some red tape at the checkpoint that delayed him, but they let him through, although they disked him in—and out, when, later, he retraced his route. Something new. The guard said it was because of runaways. They had instructions to be extra careful. Laddie had started back later than he'd intended and was overtaken by nightfall. After a spill that could have broken his neck, when he hit a pothole he didn't see, he decided it was too dangerous to continue to ride at night, given the conditions of the highway. He'd have to walk his bike, though he still had ten miles to go. It was midnight when he got home.

He found a note on his pillow.

"Dear Laddie— It's my turn to attend religious meeting tomorrow, and I want you and Greta to come with me. Please don't say no. Mom."

Attendance of progeny was optional, but it was obligatory for one adult from each household to go to the meetings on either Saturday or Sunday each week, because the meetingmasters almost always came with official announcements or with forms that had to be filled out. Laddie wrote on the back of the note, "I'll come only if Greta doesn't come with us," and left it on the kitchen table.

When he got up the next morning, he found the note pushed back under the door. His mother had added, "I want both of my kids with me."

When he came downstairs, he said to her, "You'll have to choose, Mom. Greta or me. You can't have us both. It's a familiar situation, right?"

His mother looked off as she felt her way through the meaning behind his words and the way he'd said them. Then she said sadly, "In that case I choose you, Laddie."

☐

They took the bicycles, although Louise didn't ride very well, because the meeting place was too distant for her to walk. They went slowly down Bentham Road and turned onto Riccardo, passing a fair number of inhabited dwellings at first, but toward the end of Riccardo, and especially after they turned onto Mill Road, there were mostly ghost houses.

"It seems like there are more ghosts every time I go

to meeting," Louise said. "Soon there won't be enough people living out here to keep our mile active. They'll all of a sudden declare it closed, and we won't have any place to live."

"Since you see it coming, you should move now, Mom."

"Should is different from can," she said.

"Mom, I've had a lot of time to think these last few days, and I have to talk to you about something. About Greta. She's changing, Mom. Changing fast. I don't think you and Dad realize it, but step back and look. Because it's like the ghost houses in our mile. Like that, it's something you'd be better off not having to face suddenly. And don't think I'm saying this because Greta gets to stay and I have to go away. I'm not. I'm saying it because I care what happens here even though I won't be here to—to see it."

"Greta's upset because you're going away."

"Why do you say that when you know it's not true?"

"And . . . I think she's going through a stage. She's going through a . . . a naughty stage. You did the same thing. It's natural."

"I'm not so sure there's *anything* all that natural about Greta."

"Don't talk like that."

"Don't keep denying what's so obvious."

When Louise Grayson was nervous, she tended to

oversteer. "Everything's getting more and more upside down," she said, as she wobbled across the road and nearly went into the ditch.

"There's no such thing as *more* upside down. Upside down is upside down, isn't it?" Laddie called to her.

She wobbled back. "Quibble, quibble, Laddie."

"You do hear me?" Laddie said, more harshly. "*Greta is getting out of hand.* You and Dad are going to have to do something about it. I won't be here to help." He allowed a pause. "*As* you know."

"Have you spoken to him?"

"Why bother? He wouldn't listen. I don't know what's wrong with her, Mom, but it's not a phase, in the way you mean it anyway. I think it's more . . . serious. That thing she did last week at the Pratts' contamination procedure, it was the last straw." Laddie remembered the incident at the pond. "Almost. Do *you* believe me, that she tripped Sam?"

"I don't know what to believe anymore." Louise cycled on, weaving back and forth. When they were within sight of the meeting place, she stopped a moment. "Pray it *is* a phase. I mean, pray this morning. They'll have all those official prayers, but don't say them. Pray to yourself, please let it be that Greta's going through a phase that she'll grow out of. Pray hard, Laddie. As hard as you can."

"If I pray all *that* hard, Mom," he said, "I'll pray for

myself. Nobody else will." He shoved down on his right pedal and surged ahead toward the bike rack.

☐

The meeting was in the former restaurant of an abandoned motel, the rest of which, crumbling into rubbish, had been posted off limits and sealed up. There were only minimal facilities—a few light bulbs in the chandeliers and in the wall fixtures, and a couple of heaters for cold weather. No running water. They'd dug the holes for an outhouse in the midst of the stumps of shrubbery that had been eaten to the ground by deer and rabbits before they were starved out.

When Laddie and his mother arrived, the mistress of the meeting—it was a woman that day—was already up at the lectern in front of the assembled citizens, who were seated on rickety jump chairs. Laddie saw George Vibert with his mother and father and his younger sister, Lily, who was Greta's age. Joey was there, too, with his mother and father, and his sister Flor.

The meetingmistress went through the general services. Sometimes additional special services were tacked on—Jewish on Saturday, Catholic, Mormon, Baptist, and the like, on Sunday—but this Sunday was nondenominational. First were prayers, including Our Parent, who art in heaven, and a couple of nonspecific hymns, then the announcements.

There would be a special issue of ascorbic acid for ages five to forty-five to compensate for the anticipated lack of citrus fruit coming in from SOUSEC. Nobody in the outlying miles was to pick any wild berries as they became ripe because of the danger of toxic molds. The service closed with a special prayer for the harvest and with a harvest hymn, "Bringing in the Sheaves." Then, before anyone could leave, the meetingmistress announced that she had something important to say about the progeny program, specially directed to families involved in the program, but everyone should remain and hear it.

She spoke of how the program should be taken as a positive thing. There were unwarranted rumors about it and far too much unjustified resentment. There had been cases reported in which the magistrates in charge of the hearings had been verbally abused, in one instance physically assaulted. There had also been program-connected runaways. "In their concern over this development, the Council has inaugurated prevention procedures. Any progeny unwise enough to consider running away should be warned of its special dangers now, but that is really not the point. Rather, the progeny who are going away in the program should look on it as the chance for a better life, a chance to make something more of themselves. Parents should think of their progeny, severed forever though they may be, as having been given a great opportunity. They should not think of the loss, but of the gain." She stopped. Her voice faltered. She began to cry.

"I am myself losing a child, my friends," she said. "A girl. She's only thirteen. The light of my life, though I love my ten-year-old son, too." She couldn't go on for a moment.

Others were by then crying. Louise. Maria Hernandez.

The meetingmistress pulled herself together. "Come. We must have courage. Let's all sing the first two verses of hymn number thirty. For the progeny we will be losing."

They concluded with a fervent "Oh hear us when we cry to Thee, for those in peril on the sea." Louise, an anguished look on her face, whispered to Laddie, "If only we could believe what she said before."

"Why should we when she obviously doesn't?" Laddie said.

People began to leave. As Joey Hernandez's father stamped past the Graysons, he muttered to Louise, "If I *could* think happy thoughts about the program, *that* woman wouldn't make me do it. I wish I knew how to start a revolution."

His wife hushed him and pushed him on. Laddie went

out right behind them and began to talk to Joey. George Vibert came up.

"The shed. This afternoon. Four o'clock," George said. "I'll have something for you guys. My pickup is tomorrow, and I don't want to leave my family for long, so be on time."

The Hernandez family left. Louise hadn't appeared. Laddie checked the bicycle stand, to make sure she hadn't come out a side door. Not there either, and both their bicycles were still in place. He went back inside and found her still seated on her chair.

"Come sit beside me a minute, Laddie." He edged in next to her, and she put an arm around him and pulled him close to her. "Don't ever think, Laddie, that just because I worry about Greta so much, and so much about my own aches and pains, I won't worry about you when you've gone."

"I know you will. For a while."

"Forever. You must believe that, Laddie."

"Mom, I've noticed you walking. Your back and your hips are getting worse, aren't they? Getting worse faster, I mean." Louise nodded, wordlessly. "You and Greta, you're both getting worse faster, only in different ways. It's like you're on the same timetable."

Louise stared at him. "What do you mean by that?"

"Nothing. It was just an . . . observation."

"I can do without your observations."

"Then let me ask a question. Is there a lot of arthritis in your family?"

"I don't know about my parents. They died so young. Your great-grandmother Ladd was still limber when I went out to see her at the end. Her heart was bad, but she was still spry. I don't think my grandfather Ladd limped or anything like that. That's as much as I know. Are you worried about yourself?"

"Yeah, sure. That's why I asked, Mom."

"You're lying, but I'm not going to pursue it. Because I have something I want to say that's *important.* I still feel it was the right thing to do. To keep Greta with us. But also I want to say that your feelings shouldn't be hurt and you shouldn't think we don't love you *at least* as much as we love her. But your father's right. You have to take care of people who are weak."

"Greta is *mean*, Mom, not weak. Greta is really mean. The day is going to come when you'll wish you'd got rid of her when you had the chance."

"That's a terrible thing to say. It's like you're cursing us—and her."

"Someone in our family's got to try to see things the way they really are. And maybe I have the right to say something terrible. Maybe I have a right to curse . . . someone."

☐

When Laddie and his mother got home, Arthur Grayson was waiting for them out in the road. He was very agitated. "Where have you been? What's taken you so long? Greta's run away," he said. "I can't find her anywhere. I've been going up and down the road, calling for her. She had a kind of—kind of tantrum. I shook her. Not hard. God knows, I didn't do it hard. She ran out of the house. I don't know where she is."

"She'll be at the pond," Laddie said.

"Why would she go to the pond?" Louise said.

"Because she's not supposed to."

"You see?" Arthur said to Louise. "He does pick at her."

"Pick at her or not, it's where she likes to go the most. She's kind of—kind of *crazy*—you get me?—where the pond is concerned. You ought to know that. For future reference."

"Go get her," Arthur Grayson said. "I don't want to face her again just yet. She screamed such . . . threats at me."

"Like what?"

"It doesn't matter. She didn't mean them."

"Like *what*, Dad?"

"Like that thing she said after your mother fainted. Now please go get her, Laddie."

Greta wasn't out on the dam. She was at the place up at the shallow end of the pond, wading in water over her knees. Laddie rolled up his pants and went in after her. She came along without fighting him back, as if it didn't matter now. She didn't eat lunch or speak to anyone. Arthur Grayson offered her a piece of synsweet if she'd say just one word. Any word. But she refused.

9

George Vibert arrived at the shed with a piece of paper in his hand. "It's a list of phrases that will sound natural inserted in a letter home," he explained. "I'll tell my family, also you guys, where I am by using them."

"Hey! Good idea," Joey said.

"I figured, why not let everybody know if I can. But since they'll probably read our mail, it has to be code, right?"

Laddie and Joey looked at the list. "I'm feeling fine" stood for Africa. 'Feeling just fine' stood for South America.

Laddie said, "That'll be nice to know, but I'd be more

interested in some general impressions of the program. Including maybe ones you wouldn't want to tell your parents."

That was all right with George. They worked out another system that ranked his impression of the program from excellent to poor, based on the way he wrote the salutation to his first letter. Excellent was, 'Hi, folks!' Poor was 'Dear Mom, Dear Dad.'

"I think there should be one more," Laddie said. "For disaster. I mean, if you think it's practically a death sentence, why don't you write, 'Dear Mom, Dear Dad, Dear Lily'?" Lily Vibert's name hadn't appeared in the other code salutations.

"Won't that get flagged? Too many 'dears'?" Joey asked.

Laddie said, "He has a sister and she's dear to him, right? Some people have more luck than others."

"Okay. Add it," George said. "Though I'm not going to need it." He memorized the new list, then gave it to Laddie. He shook hands with Joey. "You're next. Have fun. Good luck." He grinned. "See you in Tahiti."

Laddie, when George turned to him, prolonged their handshake a moment. "I was beginning to think you weren't a loyal Smart Rat anymore, but you are. So— here's Ratpower to you."

"Thanks. Although I'm not going to need *it* either."

That night Greta disappeared again. Normally nobody went into her room once she was asleep for fear of awakening her, but Louise checked on her, because of her strange earlier behavior, and found her bed empty. Then Louise discovered that the door that opened from the upstairs hall onto a small balcony and an outside stairway to the backyard was slightly ajar.

"She'll be at that pond again," Laddie said. "That's why she came back so easily earlier today. She was already planning to go back again after dark. I'm not going to go and get her alone. You'd better learn how. Bring the flashlight, Dad."

Greta was out on the dam. Her mother and father called to her. She wouldn't come. When Laddie started out to bring her back, she turned to him, ready this time.

He stayed out of her range. "You're a pain in the ass," he said, so only she could hear. "And you *deserve* whatever happens to you." He turned back. "I can't get her. I'm afraid to try."

"*Afraid?*" Arthur said, shocked. "Afraid of Greta? Well I'm not. I'll get her."

"Let her stay there, Dad."

Louise said, "Laddie may be right, Art. Let's wait her out."

"Certainly *not!*" Arthur went forward, feeling his way with one foot.

Louise shone the flashlight on the surface of the dam in front of him. "Why are you afraid, Laddie?" she said.

"She did this before. When I went after her, she tried to drown me."

"Are you . . . sure?"

"Mom, do you think I'd say it if I weren't?"

"Then . . . go out behind him so you can help if he needs it. Hurry, Laddie."

Laddie didn't move. "I don't necessarily think that three drownings are better than two," he said coldly.

"Laddie, what's happened to you?"

"Think about it."

As Arthur approached her, Greta turned, jumped the spillway, almost lost her balance, recovered, got to the far end of the dam, and once she was on firm ground, bolted for the house. Louise ran after her and went into her bedroom to talk to her. When she came back downstairs, there was blood in the corner of her mouth.

"She hit me," she whispered. Her voice went up. "With her fist. As hard as she could."

"She's in a mood," Arthur said, wearily. "She's overtired."

"Since when do you hit your own mother just because you're overtired? What are we going to do, Art?" Louise wailed.

"I have to go to work tomorrow. I'm going to bed."

"That's one way of dealing with a catastrophe," Laddie said.

"Let's not exaggerate, Laddie," Arthur said.

10

Arthur Grayson was obliged to be present at George Vibert's pickup. Joey and Laddie went too, of course. The van that arrived was much like the one that had taken away the Pratts, and members of the Law Enforcement Corps were in charge of the pickup procedure, too. There were already several teenage male progeny in the van when it got to the Viberts' a little before nine o'clock. They were not allowed to get out.

The Viberts lived in an antique trailer home, situated on a piece of land so slanted that six steps were needed to reach the little porch. Mr. and Mrs. Vibert and George's sister, Lily, kissed him good-bye up at the door when the van arrived, then waited there to watch the rest of the procedure.

The lieutenant in charge said, "Where is the milemaster?" Arthur handed him George's documents. The lieutenant read the name, then said, "George Vibert, come forward." George stepped forward, his small suitcase in his hand. "This is George Vibert?" the lieutenant asked Arthur. Arthur said it was. To George the lieutenant said, "You've brought only what you were told you could bring? Nothing more?" George nodded. The lieutenant turned to a corpsman, who was standing by. "Mark him," he said.

The corpsman was carrying an ink pad and a stamp. He put purple *P*'s, approximately one and a half inches in length, on George's cheeks and forehead, and on the back of each of his hands.

"The *P*, that's for progeny. Indelible. Won't come off for six months—just in case you should think of trying something," the lieutenant said. "Get in the van."

George climbed in and sat down. The corpsmen took their places in guard cages, the lieutenant joined the driver inside the front cage. The van started up. As it pulled off, Laddie gave the Smart Rats sign. George ignored it.

Arthur left for work on his bicycle. Laddie and Joey walked home together. They didn't say much, but both of them were thinking the same thing.

It had been like a criminal procedure. They had treated George like someone condemned to deportation.

☐

Later in the day Laddie took the other bicycle and went to the Center. He checked the balcony. No feet. He went to Barbara's door and rang the bell. Nobody answered.

He went on to the information outlet, which was in a building located close to the rat nets that separated the old city from the inhabited areas, and which contained the public library, a small museum, the knowledge services office, and the religious office. Laddie took a corridor that went past the museum, a large room where men were at work installing an exhibition, and led to the reading room of the library.

Reading at a desk in the center of the room sat the librarian, who looked up when Laddie approached. He held out a hand. "Your disk, please." Laddie gave it to him and he inserted it into a receptor. "What are you here for?" he asked.

"To do some reading," Laddie replied.

"About what?"

"Ecology and stuff like that."

"Your reasons?"

"Curiosity, I guess."

"Curiosity isn't an acceptable objective. Be more specific."

"I'm in the new progeny relocation program. They say we're going to subequatorial disinhabited areas to reclaim them, so I thought while I wait for my pickup date I'd read up on the problems they had before they were abandoned."

The librarian entered the information, then pointed to an alcove. "Environmental disasters are over there. You can browse all you want, but if you decide to *read* you must pass the book by me so I can note its title."

The hunch that had brought Laddie to the library didn't suggest exactly what to look for or where to find it. He scanned the indexes of a couple of books without any particular luck, then came on a series of volumes that looked as if they might be useful: the annual reports of the International Committee for the Ecological Crisis. He turned to the introduction of volume I, which was dated March 21, 2016.

"It was during the final decades of the twentieth and the first decade and a half of this century that the earth's capacity to support its proliferating human population was first impaired, then overwhelmed. As a result, ecological deterioration such as deforestation, algal tides, estuarial eutrophy, desertification, pelagic, terrestrial, and atmospheric pollution of every kind, aggravated by climatic changes that resulted from modifications of the atmosphere, set the stage for the crisis that is now everywhere in evidence."

All that was too general. Laddie consulted the index and found a reference to the effects of chemical pollutants on the health of the general population—a good place to start. After he took the book to the librarian to record, Laddie sat down and opened to the entry. It was concerned with pollutants of all kinds, but its chief subject was the then new toxicant Destron.

"Recently added to the dangerous toxic substances that are being released into the environment is Destron. First marketed in 2009, it has quickly superseded almost all other compounds of its type, except for a few that are still used for such special purposes as the control of body parasites on humans and domestic animals. Licensed by its parent company, it is sold, often with some small variations in its structure, under various names: Kilkwik, Countdown, Rout, Finale, among many others. Mixed with a special lure, it is called R.A.T., an acronym for Rodent Annihilation Toxin (the claim implied by the name has by no means been substantiated). Promoted by certain international chemical companies as an answer to the criticisms made by ecologists of existing herbicidal, pesticidal, and fungicidal substances, it has quickly proven itself by far the most dangerous and unpredictable in its effects on plant and animal life, including serious physiological and neurological damage to human beings. Later reports will note the damage it is inflicting as more becomes known about it."

Laddie sensed he was on the track. Excited now, he put that volume back and, flipping pages hastily, looked at the others in the series—the latest dated 2027, the year in which the committee had been abolished. Therein he found what he wanted, so succinctly stated he could read it standing on his feet.

"The subcommittee appointed to study the effects of Destron has completed its investigation. We summarize here the highlights of the report.

"Destron has proved to be a very dangerous substance, of high toxicity, quite various in its effects, and very persistent. An adult human being exposed to a large enough amount dies within about twenty-four hours, from destruction of the red blood corpuscles and asphyxiation resulting from the loss of motor control of the diaphragm. This effect has been observed repeatedly in areas such as Central America and Southeast Asia, where safety regulations are commonly ignored by landowners, peasants, and governments alike. Absorbed in a less than fatal dose, Destron damages its victim more slowly. It seems to have a particular predilection for the following areas and organs: nervous tissue, including the brain; sperm; ova; and the skeleton and joints (see section two for further particulars). It has also been reported to have caused blindness and deafness."

Laddie read on until he found information about the effects of Destron on the human skeleton.

"Direct exposure during infancy will frequently lead to malformations of the hands and feet and of the spine; also, the normal development of the cranium may be affected (for prenatal exposure, see paragraph H below). In older individuals, the most common symptom is much like arthritis, and like arthritis, is progressive and incurable; unlike arthritis, it progresses rapidly in its later stages."

Laddie raised his head and shaded his eyes a moment as he thought of his mother. It all fit. He skipped down to paragraph H.

"Destron is now known to be extremely toxic to the human fetus." There followed the case history of a male infant exposed to Destron before birth who developed normally for several years, then, at age eight, began to exhibit personality and behavioral disorders. By ten the boy had become uncontrollably violent and had to be institutionalized. "Any pregnant woman who is exposed to Destron," the report stated, "would be prudent to have an abortion at once. Further tests, to determine the extent of her absorption of the substance, will help to determine whether or not she should ever again allow herself to be fertilized."

Laddie closed the book. He now knew enough. And it

was all so obvious he was surprised he hadn't come here to find it out before.

As he was leaving, the librarian asked him, in a kindly way, "When is your pickup date?" Laddie replied it was October 26. "We'll have our new exhibition up in the museum before then. Come back and see it. They're working on it right now. It's about the disinhabited areas. A lot about rats." The librarian gave a wry little smile. "About rats and I suppose *other* agreeable vermin."

11

When Laddie got home, he found his mother sitting outside in the sun; the ozone report continued good for NORSEC. He sat down beside her.

"Mom, I want to ask you about something. Yesterday you mentioned going out to see Granny Ladd. I'm interested in that trip. I remember your going, and I remember your telling Dad and me when you got back about what went wrong on the way, but I don't remember details, exactly. It was ten years ago, right? So I was only seven?"

Louise nodded. "That terrible trip. I don't like to think about it."

"Your bus broke down, isn't that what you said? In

California somewhere? And people died?"

"Near ex-Sacramento." Louise Grayson turned very slowly toward him, her eyes suspicious. *"Why do you want to know?"*

"Well, I'm going away myself, only I'll never come back. I'd kind of like to have some family stories to think about."

"You would? That doesn't sound exactly like you, Laddie."

"Circumstances have changed, Mom. Please tell me."

"Well, all right." Louise told him how the news had come that his great-grandmother Ladd, who lived out in NORWESEC, was sick. She'd raised Louise Grayson, whose mother and father had died in California during the earthquakes. Mrs. Ladd had found Louise in one of the refuges set up in Idaho and had taken her home. Now she was dying, and Louise didn't want her to die all alone. She'd managed to get space on a bus. The trip took twelve days.

"Leaving me with Dad, I remember that," Laddie said. "But what about Greta?"

"Do a little subtraction. She wasn't here yet."

"Pretty close to it. Were you pregnant at the time, Mom?"

"Well, yes. I didn't know it." Louise smiled. "Your father and I didn't exactly *plan* to have another baby right then, but we didn't exactly *not* plan to either. As it turned out, I was in my third week when I left."

"You said you were near ex-Sacramento. What was the landscape like?"

"Flat. Some huge agricultural business had been there before they abandoned it. The buildings were still standing. And farm machinery."

"They would have used a lot of chemicals. Pesticides. All that. Were there pollution warning signs, Mom?"

Louise nodded. "Lots of them. Our bus had special filters, I remember. Anyway, the ventilating system stopped when the engine did. So did the air-conditioning. It was three o'clock on a July afternoon. Hot. I never saw such heat. The driver radioed for help to the nearest center. None came for almost six hours—during which the temperature slowly coasted down from a hundred and twenty-two degrees in the shade. Can you believe it? They told us that was actually *sub*normal for the Central Valley of California after its desertification. We had to get out of the bus, of course. Two people died of heat-stroke. All of us were sick. For one thing, we ran out of water."

"Why didn't the rescue team come sooner?"

"We never found out. I was too sick to care."

"Were you tested or treated for—for Destron exposure, let's say?"

"They had us breathe into something. They said not to be worried. They said the area we'd broken down in hadn't been contaminated in years."

"I wonder why they left the signs up, then."

"Probably because nobody wanted the bother of taking them down."

"What did the report say?"

"There wasn't ever any report about the incident. They took away the two passengers who died of heatstroke and gave us a new bus, and that was that."

"They covered up. I'll bet it would have been a punishable offense to have left you out there for so long."

"Anyway, I went to the exchange point and caught another bus that went north. Eventually, I got to Wolf Creek, in Oregon, where Granny Ladd lived. She was a really remarkable woman, Laddie. If you want stories, there are a lot of them I can tell you about her. Like the time she went out of her house and personally told the Council housing condemner that if he condemned her house she was going to— Laddie, you aren't listening to me."

"I don't care so much about that part, Mom."

"You don't want to hear about your grandmother's death? It was *very* dignified, Laddie. Something to be proud of. It's the *important* part of the story, as far as I'm concerned." Louise stood up and looked down at him. "What's this all about? What are you trying to prove?"

"Sometimes, Mom, it's better to know what you're up against than to hide from it."

"Hide from it? Hide from what?"

"I think you already know."

"I do *not* already know *anything.* What are you trying to do to me?"

"Nothing that may not have been done already."

Louise screamed, "Stop it. You're turning into someone I don't recognize. Stop it." She tried to run back into the house.

Laddie watched her. She stopped twice when her hip hurt her too much to continue. Slowly, he shook his head, his feelings numbed by the hopelessness of his family's situation.

□

"Louise," Arthur called. "Oh, my God, Louise." He dropped his bike in the driveway and hurried into the house. "Laddie, you should hear this, too. Something has happened."

There'd been an interrogation at the dry-goods distribution outlet. Arthur was doing the inventory of stationery supplies and had entered seven stapling machines. The previous weekly inventory had listed nine, and there'd been none issued in the meantime. The computer sounded an alarm, which went not only to the supervisor's desk but also down to the offices at the center. The resident had sent an interrogator immediately.

"She wasn't more than twenty-three or -four, but she was even worse than the older one who came on the Pratt case. She questioned everyone, but especially me." Arthur sat down in the kitchen and put his face in his hands. "She knew everything about us. Brought up everything on my record. The progeny hearing when you yelled at the magistrate, she mentioned that, Louise. That there was one domestic unit not represented at the Pratt procedures. She said maybe we were noncooperative. She even hinted—she hinted maybe I'd been in on a deal of some kind with Lewis Pratt. She said she'd never thought that investigation had gone far enough. While all this was going on, they'd put an antagonist team into the storeroom and they found the stapling machines behind a carton of paper clips." Arthur looked up at his wife and at his son. "What will we do?"

"Calm down, Dad," Laddie said. "After all, they found them."

"That doesn't matter," Arthur moaned. "Once something like this gets going, they never leave off. They'll find some reason. I'll be sentenced for Trade and Barter. You'll be sentenced, too, Louise. Laddie won't, because he'll be gone. And Greta because she's too young." Arthur looked around. "Where *is* Greta?"

"I'm right here," Greta said. She'd been standing at

her usual place in the hallway, eavesdropping.

"Forget everything I just said, honey," Arthur said.

"Why should I?" Greta said. She skipped out to the kitchen. "I'm hungry, hungry, hungry, hungry, hungry."

"There she goes again," Louise said. "I can't *stand* it."

"Give her a cracker," Arthur said. "We don't want her getting mad again. You'll be the lucky one, Laddie. You'll be safe off somewhere nice and warm. Better anywhere than here. You'll thank us for choosing you, before you're through."

REDUCTION
AND
RELOCATION

12

The Progeny Reduction and Relocation Program, once George Vibert was fully inducted into it, quickly redefined his optimistic worldview.

Item. The first night. About a hundred boys his age from all over NORSEC were placed in the gymnasium of a disused school in what had formerly been a rural education district. The Enforcement Corps locked the doors and posted guards outside. All that the hungry progeny were given to eat were foodbars for dinner and for breakfast the next day, each one rated at three hundred calories. When they were mustered outside on the playground, prior to continuing their journey, one of the boys yelled a complaint. The corps lieutenant, whom

George recognized as the Lieutenant Lindgren who'd been in charge of the Pratt deportation procedure, snapped his baton in the palm of his left hand and spoke to the sergeant, who jerked the boy forward and hit him across the mouth with his truncheon, then shoved him back into ranks. George saw the kid put his hand to his mouth and spit some teeth into it, which he kept locked up in his clenched fist all day, as if he hoped that when night came he could put them back in. By then, however, he couldn't move his lower jaw.

Item. As they drove south, they passed ex-New York, traveling on the west side of the Hudson River, where the highway, which had been designed before the general rise in the sea level, barely cleared the puddles of foul slime. Large signs stated that the entire area was dangerously polluted. All precautions should be taken against exposure to the air and the water. The driver had stopped the bus at a parking area, where she and the corpsmen put on special clothing that entirely covered their heads and bodies. They also wore masks through which they breathed. No protection of any kind was issued to the progeny, however, and the bus they were in had no filtering system. By the time the signs announced they were clear of the pollution, the skin on George's neck and forehead and around his mouth was growing red and raw, his eyes were bloodshot and swollen half shut, and he'd begun to cough.

Item. When they were checked in at the Progeny Receiving Center, they were assigned numbers, which corresponded to their places in the barracks. Their luggage was then searched. After that they were required to yield their rations disks to a representative of the Council. One of the progeny couldn't find his disk. He said it was either lost or stolen. He was taken away. What became of him was unclear.

☐

George's number was F-11, which meant that he was billeted in barracks building F, and slept at place 11. The building was identified by an "F" (from whose horizontal strokes paint had dribbled down) painted on the front door, his place inside by an "11" marked in chalk on the floor. There were no mattresses, no towels, no soap, not enough water, and very little food. The latrines quickly became disgusting undrained sewers. George spent three days without ever being allowed out of doors.

But on the morning of the fourth day he was told that he had been selected, because of his record for excellent cooperation, to be released from nine o'clock to four o'clock for cleanup detail. He was assigned to help a man named Marvin, who wore a dirty gray uniform and drove a small pickup truck. For the next three days George helped Marvin take trash from receptacles inside certain buildings and at certain locations outside as well and put it in a large general receptacle, where it was compacted. Because their duties took them beyond the boundaries of the Progeny Center, George discovered that it was only one of the area's facilities. Located roundabout were also the NORSEC Center for Incurables, the Repose Center, the Center for Psychological and Sociological Misfits, the Center for Noncooperators, and finally—surrounded by razor wire and walls and under heavy guard—the Deportation Center. George was surprised that it would have been thought appropriate to put the Repose Center, where his own grandmother had been sent two years earlier when she could no longer take care of herself, next door to the Deportation Center, where condemned criminals were held. It was as if there were no significant differences between the occupants, as if anyone who came to one of them was the same as someone at one of the others—the old, the ill, the mad, the subversive, the criminal, and the progeny in the program. George also noticed that, except for the Progeny Center, the facilities had few inmates. It occurred to him that perhaps it was not only those condemned to deportation who were shipped elsewhere.

This great composite facility lay close to an inlet from the ocean, where languid black water was sucked in and out by the tides. On his third day of cleanup duty, George's truck was sent to the heavily fenced pier that flanked the inlet. Outside the fence were receptacles into which trash from the pier had been placed, which George and Marvin dumped into their truck. Moored to the pier was the only ship George had ever seen, a ship quite different from the ones in pictures. He asked Marvin if there was any chance they'd ever get to go aboard the ship to get trash. Marvin, who didn't talk much and wouldn't often answer George's questions, said that only the officers, who had nonrationed rank, got to go aboard or leave the ship. The crew were serviles and stayed aboard twenty-four hours a day, seven days a week. George asked Marvin what a "servile" was.

"I'm a servile. Look, I'm not supposed to talk to you. If they catch me at it, I'll revert."

"Revert to what?" George asked.

"Mind your own business, for Christ's sake," Marvin said.

The next day the heavy gates to the pier were open. George could see repair trucks parked near the ship, and a lot of trash, some of it used machinery parts. Marvin was directed to move the truck up alongside the ship, and the crew tossed the trash into it so George and Marvin could take it away. The workmen who were doing the repairs, and who seemed to be from outside the centers, talked to each other in a more or less normal way, but each one had been assigned a guard, who made sure he did not talk to any of the crew. The crew, who were in uniforms like Marvin's, said nothing to one another except for commands or questions having directly to do with their tasks, and nothing to George or Marvin.

Meanwhile, as he had no hat, George's face was getting more sore every day and his lips had bleeding cracks in them. He wondered, as he palpated his eyelids, his nose, the tops of his ears, what he'd see had there been a mirror for him to look in. When he asked Marvin the day they went to the pier if he could get a hat somewhere, Marvin told him to shut up or he'd get in trouble.

"At least tell me how I look," George said.

Marvin said, "You wouldn't want to hear."

George worried about that. Skin cancer was ever on the mind of someone with his coloring. Nevertheless, it seemed to him better to be doing the work he was doing, despite the exposure to solar radiation, than to be one of the progeny who stayed in the barracks day after day, hungry, thirsty, filthy, bored, and frightened.

☐

George thought a lot about the ship. It wasn't all that big, not at all like the ones from the old days that used to cross the ocean. It had four cranes, two to a side, one forward, one aft of the bridge, which itself reared up some thirty feet amidships. Between the cranes were shallow wells into which containers, constructed of heavy metal grills, were nested. George had counted twenty of them, ten forward, ten aft, five to a side. He couldn't imagine what they were for, or why such a ship would be moored so close to the various centers.

Meanwhile, the first busloads of girls had come in. They were put in separate barracks.

Item. As George was picking up trash late in the afternoon from a building used by the Enforcement Corps that was not far from the girls' barracks, he saw male corpsmen bring a girl into the building where he was at work. She was blindfolded.

Item. Something similar happened to one of the boys in George's barracks a day later. He was taken away for an hour or two in the evening, then returned just before the lights were put out. When he was asked what had happened, he refused to tell the other boys, but he was heard to cry after dark that night, as uncontrollably as a sick baby, although he was seventeen.

☐

On the fifth day, George and Marvin were sent to the administration building and told by the corporal of the guards to sweep and clean the offices as well as remove the trash. When they were doing the floor on which were located the offices of the commandant, a colonel in the Enforcement Corps, and of the other top officers, one of the two guards assigned to watch them was called down-stairs to supervise the unloading of a truck of supplies. The other guard had to divide his time between Marvin and George. He moved constantly back and forth for a little while, but then got lazy and stayed down near the entrance to the hallway, which was the end where Marvin was working. The officers were all at a staff meeting, accompanied by their secretaries. George was alone.

As he stopped to pick up the wastebasket in the com-mandant's office, he noticed a document that had been left on the desk. Two weeks earlier it would never have occurred to him to read something addressed to some-one else, but he had no such scruples left. He pulled it out in the clear from under the blotter. It had "MAXI-MUM SECURITY" stamped on it, and was also marked as a copy; possibly the commandant had taken the origi-nal with him to the meeting then in progress. George managed, as he dusted the window sills and swept the floor, to read it through. The guard checked him only once, and the sound of footsteps in the hall on that occasion gave George plenty of time to put the docu-ment back where he'd found it.

□

"From: The Chairman of the Subcommittee for Law and Order of the Governing Council of NORSEC

"To: Commandant, Progeny Reduction Center

"Subject: Progeny Disposal Procedures

"1. The difficulties you have encountered in the execution of the progeny disposal procedures must be overcome as quickly as possible and the procedures expedited. Progeny are backing up in the system because you cannot accept them at the Reduction Center. Already the temporary holding shelters are filled to capacity. Runaways are on the increase. Should it become necessary to defer pickups, further strains on the procedures will be incurred, causing more unrest, as well as giving the opposition to the program within the Council additional opportunity for criticism.

"2. At a recent emergency meeting of the Subcommittee it was suggested that when the disposal vessel is repaired, you should shorten the distance from the mainland at which the procedure is executed by about twenty miles and thus save four hours a round trip. This would violate the inter- and intrajurisdictional antipollution treaties; however, maps of the ocean currents suggest that such a reduction would not result in any undesirable material reaching inhabited shore areas where it might foment rumors, since there are now no parts of the coast inhabited south of fifty-five degrees of latitude.

"3. When disposal schedules are again on line, you would then be able to run three trips a day, counting, if the new distance is utilized, on six hours for a round trip, which would allow the officers and servile crew six hours of sleep out of twenty-four. If the container capacity is figured at two hundred, a total of six hundred progeny each day (minus such places as might be needed for incurables, repose cases, etc; their disposal procedures must not, of course, be suspended), and each week some forty-two hundred progeny, would thereby be disposed of. If this schedule were maintained for a period of three weeks, the backlog at this end would be relieved and the disposal rate could drop back to the one anticipated in the plan.

"4. Security leaks already seem to be occurring, and the Subcommittee is apprehensive of increased unrest in the rationed population. Therefore, when the epistolary procedures are put into effect, the utmost vigilance must be exercised by the censors to make sure no secret messages get through.

"Please be assured that you have our wholehearted support in these difficult times."

☐

As George left the office, he noticed a small mirror by the door. He stopped. His face was blistered and peeling. On his nose and ears were running sores, and the skin around the purple *P*'s that had been stamped on his forehead and cheeks was blistered and oozing. He looked like someone the system was planning to throw away.

When he and Marvin were back in the truck, he said, "Marvin, what would happen to a guy who tried to run from here?"

Marvin kept his eyes straight ahead. "They'd catch him."

"What would they do to him?"

"I've heard the screaming," Marvin said. "Better forget it. Anyway, it's no better outside the fences than it is inside."

When the truck passed the waterfront on its way back to the garage, Marvin stopped a moment where a narrow gap in the buildings allowed a view through to the pier. The repair vehicles were gone and a wisp of oily smoke was coming out of the ship's smokestack. Crewmen were moving fore and aft. The cranes, turning like great birds, were lifting the heavy wire containers off the ship to place them on wheeled platforms that sat on the pier.

Before Marvin turned George over to the guard at his barracks, he said, "It's just possible they may give you the choice they gave me. I'm going to tell my supervisor what a good worker you are. When they need workers, they sometimes give condemned people the choice of becoming serviles. I was sent here for deportation, you see. I put off my deportation by doing dirty work. Turning servile. It's done other places, too. Like, the families

of deportees, who are guilty by association, become serviles at the Council Center. I just hope my wife and
daughter are there. I've got no rights, I don't get enough
to eat, I sleep at night in a cell, I never get a day off, but
at least I've never been put on that ship. Someday, when
there isn't a labor shortage, I'll revert and be rotated,
meaning I'll be deported and another man will take my
place. All I try to do is to put that day off as long as I can.
You should do the same. If they give you the chance.
Don't figure that where they're going to take you will be
better. Careful. The guard's watching us. Good luck,
George."

☐

That night George's group was informed they would be
moved to another location the following morning, the
first step in their subequatorial relocation. Each of them
was given a piece of paper and a pencil and told to write
his family no more than a hundred words. A letter that
demonstrated a positive attitude would be noted in the
data file of its author. The letters would all be analyzed
by computer. Anyone found guilty of attempting to com-
municate by some prearranged code would be punished.

George took that risk. There was nobody he could talk
to, nobody to whom he could tell what he knew, and no

way out. The only useful or hopeful or decent thing left for him to do was to try to help Laddie and Joey.

Dear Mom, Dear Dad, Dear Lily,

I'm writing to tell you that we're finally being shipped out tomorrow. We don't know where we're going, and if we did we couldn't tell you, but I'm looking forward to it. Waiting around is pretty boring, although they've given me some work to do. I don't know when I'll get the chance to write again, but until I do, I want you to know I think about you a lot.

Love,
George

The letters were collected and the lights turned out. Many of the boys got no sleep at all, such was their excitement over the events of the next day. George, of course, was among them.

□

The progeny were taken away, by groups of ten, in windowless trucks that were driven to a shed next to the pier, where the wire containers waited on the rolling platforms. The progeny were then transferred into the containers, whose bottoms proved to be solid, though their sides, made of the same tough, closely meshed wire as rat-proof nets, were not. The container doors, which slid up and down like window sashes, were dropped into place and locked and the platforms wheeled out so a cable from one of the cranes on the ship could be hooked onto it.

When all the containers were loaded aboard, the ship was edged away from the pier and out into the channel. It ran for half an hour between shores, then moved into the open sea at increased speed. Three hours later it slowed.

Each crane rotated to position over one of the cages in its sector. Crew members, walking across the tops of the containers, fixed hooks that were dropped from the crane into the eyes welded to the tops of the containers, and attached control cables to the upper edge of the sliding doors through which the progeny had been loaded, and to the bottom edge of the side opposite the doors, so the containers could be upended. The cranes then reared up, lifted the containers, rotated to left or right, and swung them clear of the sides of the ship. The ship's whistle blew, whereupon the brakes on the cables were released and the containers allowed to splash into the water to a depth of twenty feet. After ten minutes, the whistle blew again. The cables to the container doors were pulled to lift them open. The cables on the far sides were also pulled, so that the containers tilted, their open sides down, as they were raised out of the water, dripping—and empty. They were then nested back in their slots and the cranes moved into position for the next containers.

A few large fish had approached the ship. Now and then one of them would turn on its side and wrench at something in the water. Only the sudden descent of another container drove them away, and then only until that container, too, had spent its allotted minutes underwater and been emptied and hoisted aloft and put back in its place.

When the disposal procedure was completed, the ship returned to the pier, where more progeny were waiting.

□

The clerk came in, bowed, and informed the censor that twenty more letters were ready.

The censor summoned them up on her monitor, one after the other, read them, approved them, and passed them on. When the seventeenth came up, the computer beeped an alarm.

She questioned it.

EXPLANATION NECESSARY FOR LILY AND EXCESSIVE REPETITIONS OF DEAR IN LINE ONE.

The censor got the billet number of the progeny who'd written the letter off the envelope and keyboarded it into the computer. She scanned F-11's info file, which had been transferred into the Enforcement Corps computer system at the time the rations disks were invalidated, and discovered that F-11 had a sister named Lily, also that according to his psychological evaluation, he was passive and dependent on his family.

That would explain all the sentiment.

The censor approved the letter and put the signature into the computer's graphic memory so it could reproduce it on command, and also entered a note to the effect that when the correspondence simulation procedure was put into effect, the same salutation should be used, in order to reinforce the credibility of whatever text was sent.

13

Mrs. Vibert, soft-spoken and amiable, welcomed Laddie into the house and gave him George's letter. Lily Vibert had been sent to tell him of its arrival. "We're just as pleased as punch," Mrs. Vibert said, as Laddie read the letter through.

" 'Dear Mom, Dear Dad, Dear Lily,' " he quoted.

"Wasn't it nice of George to include Lily *especially*? The program doesn't sound bad at all, does it?"

"No, Mrs. Vibert, it doesn't sound bad at all."

"I hope George gets sent somewhere where there are mountains. I've always wished I could travel and see mountains. Here's Joey. Good. Lily got to you, too. Let him read the letter, Laddie. We're just as pleased as punch, Joey."

As Joey read the letter, Mrs. Vibert said, "George mentions writing again. His father and I think they'll relent about all that. Actually, to tell you the truth, and it's probably bad luck to say it, we expect to have him back in a year or so. I mean, for a visit. I expect he won't want to *leave* the place he's going to. George likes to finish something he starts. Doesn't this make you boys eager to go yourselves? Now just doesn't it?"

□

As they walked away together, Joey said, "There can't be any doubts about it, can there? Three *Dears*? The worst?"

"No doubts at all," Laddie said. "It sure raises some questions. What do we do next?"

When they were in front of his house, Joey looked up toward the door, then at the mailbox still lying on the ground. "I promised I wouldn't, promised my dad, but I'm going to tell you something, Laddie. I'm going to run for it. This letter from George has clinched it." Joey kicked the box into the ditch. "Dad's found a truck driver at the transportation outlet where he works who's agreed to meet me west of here and take me on from there. He knows drivers in SOUCENSEC who make runs to the southwest. They'll get me to MEXSEC. Once I'm there I can find plenty of Hernandez relatives. Word about me's being passed along the grapevine."

"It's risky, Joey. They're clamping down."

"I know. But I'll be okay. Laddie, I asked my dad to ask the driver if two guys could travel together. He says no. But if you go to my dad after I've left, I know he'll try to make an arrangement of the same kind for you."

"I can't do it, Joey."

"You can't stay here. If George says it's desperate, it really must be."

Laddie told Joey about the incident of the missing items at the dry-goods distribution outlet. "They're on Dad's tail. If I run away, it'll be one more thing and could easily start up a criminal investigation. If that happens—"

"You've got a while. See how things go. Think it over."

Laddie shook his head. "It's just not for me."

Joey raised his left hand and made the sign. "Smart Rats don't give up," he said.

"Maybe if they're really smart, that's *just* what they do."

□

On Sunday, while his family was at religious meeting, Joey took a few things, strapped them to his bicycle, and set out. He left a note saying that he'd gone to the Center and wouldn't be back until evening. By then, when his parents "discovered" he wasn't coming back, it would be too late to report his absence until Monday morning. That gave him twenty-four hours.

He rode to a junction point east of the Hudson, where he hid the bicycle, then walked to a mile marker already agreed upon. He waited. The truck came less than an hour later. Joey jumped in beside the driver. They crossed the river with no difficulties. The guard ran Joey's disk through to make sure it was valid, asked Joey what he was doing, smirked when Joey said he was going to visit a woman he knew at Local Center 3, and sent them on. On Monday morning Joey moved inside the truck. His father would have gone by then to report his absence to Arthur Grayson, and Mr. Grayson would have to report him as missing as soon as he could get to an office. They'd cancel Joey's disk immediately, on the assumption that he'd run away.

Tuesday night, just before they reached the border between NORSEC and SOUCENSEC, the truck developed engine trouble. The driver managed to bring it into the next truck stop, but the mechanic there told him it couldn't go on. The cargo was perishable, so the transportation manager had the load detached from the cab and hooked up to another cab. The driver had to stay with his own cab. That was the regulation. He didn't know the driver of the new cab, but he asked the woman who manned the diesel pump, whom he knew and trusted, if the new driver was a good guy. The woman thought he might be. He complained a lot about the Council and all that. Joey's driver approached the new driver, who said sure, he'd take the kid along. It wasn't all that unusual an arrangement; truck drivers helped runaways whenever they could.

Half an hour later the truck started for the border, which was on the Ohio River. When it reached the checkpoint, the new driver jumped out of his cab and went into the guardhouse and gave them his papers.

"And I've got another one for you in the back of the truck," he said. "Male. About seventeen. Unarmed."

The guards called reinforcements in from the roadway, opened the truck, and went after Joey. When he was in custody, the corporal in charge gave the truck driver his receipt, which entitled him to double ration points for one month.

14

Colonel Kent, chief of the Internal Security Unit of the NORSEC Enforcement Corps, told the middle-aged servile who'd just brought in the big box of spare parts to put it on the general's table. "Now take his chair and upend it," Kent said. The servile did so. The officers inspected the swivel mechanism. "There's where it came from, all right," Kent said, pointing to an empty hole. He examined the thread of the screw the general had found on the floor a few minutes earlier. "No good anymore. We'll have to find a replacement, General."

Both the general and the colonel had desk chairs that had mechanisms that permitted them not only to swivel but also to tip back. Real antiques, at least a hundred

years old, which Colonel Kent had found two years earlier in an abandoned office building in the woods outside
ex-Harrisburg, where he'd gone on a hunt for runaways.
Intrigued, he'd brought them back and offered one to his
general. Nothing like the chairs had been made since the
troubles. All you could get now was a model that came
from SOUWESEC that didn't even swivel properly,
much less tip at the same time. In order to keep the
antiques functioning—he repaired them himself—the
colonel had to maintain a reserve of spare parts, culled
from junkyards and abandoned offices throughout the
region.

He and the general looked into the box and found the
plastic bag that contained screws. Colonel Kent dumped
them out on top of the desk.

"Won't that one do?" the general said.

"Let's try it, sir."

While he watched Kent fit the screw into the hole from
which the stripped screw had dropped, the general
talked business.

"New program's not going any too smoothly, Kent.
Not our problem, to be sure. Problem of the Special
Detachment. We have to help, of course. They can't
move the progeny through the tube, so to speak. Break-
down in the disposal procedures."

The colonel, a slim man with long, quick fingers, was
having difficulties of his own. The screw didn't fit.

"Doesn't seem to want to go, does it?" The general examined the screws on his desk again. "Here's one that will go better, I think." He handed another screw to the colonel, which did fit, though only more or less.

As he inserted it, the colonel said, "You were saying, sir?"

"Logistical difficulties with the progeny program aren't the whole story. Lot of rationed unrest showing up. We're pretty quiet here in NORSEC, but I understand there's been something damn close to an uprising in NORCENSEC." The general leaned forward. "Good. Good. That's going to do it, isn't it?" He straightened up again. "They're having to crack down. Hard."

"It'll do it for a while, sir. I don't claim the repair is long-term."

"What is? One form the unrest is taking everywhere is a sharp increase in the number of runaways. Have her put the chair on its feet, Kent. I'd better give it a good try before she puts the parts box back."

The colonel gave the command to the servile, who turned the chair over. The general sat down, swiveled, tipped back and forth, then spun in a full circle. All was well.

"You may return the box to my closet and go back to your cleaning," the colonel told the servile. He sat down on the straight chair next to the general's desk. "Runnies can't be a serious problem," he said. "Unarmed and hungry kids? Hardly a threat to the system."

The general said, "Some of them got weapons in SOUCENSEC. They held up a distribution outlet, using them. Actually murdered a couple of corpsmen. We've got things under better control. All the same, the proliferation of runnies is a problem. And the rumors! Security leaks, too. There's still plenty of opposition to the program at the highest level. It may be that there are leaks there. The President of the Council and, more important for us, the Chairman of the Subcommittee for Law and Order, are worried. A rise in the number of runnies could slow things down. Lead to more unrest among the rationed citizenry. Call for deployment of security forces. Once a kid has run away, the cat's out of the bag. We have to stop and hunt and all that. People see us. People see them. People hear about them. Some of them will escape to MEXSEC, inevitably. They're very uncooperative down there. I hear their progeny program is a joke. Their usual inefficiency. Anyway, word will get back. We'll have anarchy."

"Bad show, sir."

"Our best bet is to stop runnies before they go. One way to do this is to increase the favorable propaganda about the progeny program. They're sending second rounds of letters home from the progeny that have already been taken off. A selection is going to be printed up and circulated. So that's the carrot, to make the progeny go quietly, and keep their families quiet, too. Then there's the stick. That's where we come in."

"You bet it is, sir."

"We've got to convince people that to run away is almost certain death—or worse."

The general tipped back and watched the serviles who were tending the lawns. "The threat of exposure to cold isn't all that effective this time of year. As for starvation—well, they're used to that. However, we have one trump card. The Chairman of the Subcommittee and I have decided that henceforth all runnies we capture will have been mauled by rats, the smart ones who work in packs. *You* know, Kent." The general smiled a little. "Smart rats are getting more and more out of control. Getting smarter. If that isn't known now, it soon will be. No runny can get by them. We want people to *see* that for themselves. You get me?"

"Why won't the runnies themselves say there are practically no rats left?"

"Because they won't be able to talk, Colonel. I leave the rest up to you."

As the general tipped forward, something went clink. Both officers looked on the floor. The replacement screw had already dropped out.

The colonel went to the door, opened it, and clapped his hands to get the attention of the general's servile.

□

Lieutenant Lyman Lindgren walked briskly into Colonel Kent's office, saluted, and stood at attention, eyes straight ahead. The colonel observed the fanatical neatness of Lindgren's uniform, the faultless cut of his hair, and the cruel thinness of his lips, then took a moment to look at Lindgren's dossier again, trying to determine from his appearance and the documents if he was the man for the job, as Lindgren's captain had suggested.

"Take a chair, Lieutenant," Kent then said. "I want to explore a certain problem informally with you."

Half an hour later, the colonel tipped himself forward on his own double-swivel chair and put his fingertips on his desk. "I will make sure you have a supply of runnies. One every couple of days. Get in touch with my office when the one you have on hand has come to the end of his or her usefulness and we'll provide you with another, even if we have to . . . invent him. Your job is to make the demonstrations so effective that no progeny will consider taking the runaway route after seeing one of them." The colonel stood.

"This is a project close to the heart of several powerful people, Lieutenant. The Chairman of the Subcommittee on Law and Order, even the President of the Council, will hear about you, if it goes well. You will have to forgo all leave, including weekends, until it's concluded. We want you on the move day and night. Hit every floor in the high-density buildings, each cluster in medium density, each mile out in the country. If you carry out this mission with the efficiency with which you have been carrying out your assignment as Disciplinary Actions officer, I think a captaincy might well be in your future. But I'll be candid with you. We've got two other officers on similar duty. I expect to have only one captaincy to dispose of at the end of this thing."

"The good of the Sector is more important than advancement, sir," Lindgren said.

Colonel Kent nodded, bored.

"Sir, may I say one thing somewhat off the subject?" Kent nodded again, wary now. "Your chair, sir. I've heard about it from other officers. Would you show me what it can do?"

Kent smiled and sat down again. "Of course," he said. He swiveled, then tipped back, then did both simultaneously.

Lindgren gawked in amazement. "Those were certainly the good old days, weren't they, sir? When there were things like this available? Someone should write a history."

☐

The Enforcement Corps car drew up to the guardhouse at the boundary between NORSEC and SOUCENSEC, and Lieutenant Lindgren, accompanied by two specially chosen corpsmen, got out and handed the guard an authorization.

The guard put the document under a weight. "He's a little hungry, otherwise in good condition. He's back in there."

Lindgren nodded to his two corpsmen, who followed him into the room where Joey Hernandez sat, his hands tied. They hauled him to his feet and took him out to their car, a station wagon that had an armored rear compartment into which arrested persons could be locked.

They drove northeast, back toward NORSEC Center. After a short while, Lindgren said, "Stop here," at a place where a stream crossed under the highway. "Bring the instruments," he said to the corpsmen; and to the driver, "Radio for an ambulance. Law and Order priority. Emergency."

They took Joey into the sourbush, which grew very high along the waterway.

15

"Give me your attention while the subject is being pre-pared for viewing," Lieutenant Lindgren said. The ambulance had come to a stop behind his car. Two orderlies had opened the rear door and awaited his signal. He glanced irritably to his far left, ready to call for silence, but realized there was nothing to be done about the noise. It was almost certainly the subject's mother—and she hadn't even seen him yet. "We have brought the subject here, his home mile, and will take him on to as many other places as possible, so that rationed citizens can see what fate is in store for anyone who runs away.

"There are the hazards of hunger and thirst, heat and cold, disease and injury, but their effects are not what will be demonstrated to you this morning. This morning, you will see a demonstration of the damage inflicted by rats.

"We have rats under control in the inhabited areas, through constant vigilance. In the disinhabited areas, they run freely, and in packs, mean and aggressive. They are organized to a degree unknown to their ancestors in previous centuries. They well deserve their name: smart rats.

"The subject ran away four days ago. He was attacked yesterday by rats, just beyond the barriers that divide the Oxbow disinhabited area from the inhabited area here to the south. When he was first sighted, the rat attack had already begun and he was running for safety, trying to get back to this side of the barriers, but before he made it the rats cut across in front of him. The guards, who'd seen him by then, put on rat armor and went to help, but they were too late.

"The rat pack circled the subject, surrounded him, moved in to the kill. He tried to defend himself. He'd grabbed an old metal trash can lid that must have been lying on the side of the highway and held it in his left hand, using it as a shield, and he had a section of sourbush, thick as my wrist, in his right hand and was using it as a club to hit at his attackers. Rats are quick. They're almost a match for our most sophisticated weapons. And there were a lot of them. His efforts were hopeless.

"They have a practiced strategy in these cases. Some go for the Achilles tendons. Hamstring their victim. Others go for the head. Blind their victim so he can't see to defend himself, and so on. That's what they did in this case. By the time our guards got to the subject, they'd done all that and more. The guards drove them off with Rodent Annihilation Toxin—the gas form. Managed to kill two of them with it."

Lindgren nodded to a corpsman, who lifted two rats, tied together by their tails, from a box. Then Lindgren signaled the orderlies, who lifted a portable stretcher-bed out of the ambulance, flipped its feet down, and set it on the ground.

"You are all to look at the subject now. He is still alive, but he can't talk. His family should be the first to view him." Lindgren raised his voice. "All rationed citizens execute the viewing procedure," he barked out. And added, "If any of you here, including his family, knew what he was going to do before he did it and encouraged him or helped him, you'll now have the opportunity to see what your help has done."

□

The family part was messy. The corpsmen had to intervene. After that people filed by in an orderly enough fashion. The last person in line was a boy about the age of the subject. He took his time and examined the subject quite closely.

Lindgren strolled up. He poked at Joey's face with his baton. "Not too much left of that, eh?"

"It's a good lesson. If I were considering running away, this would sure convince me that I shouldn't. What a stupid move!"

Lindgren prodded the shreds of Joey's left Achilles tendon. Joey jerked, but he was firmly strapped in place. "He won't ever make a move again," Lindgren said, "stupid or otherwise."

"He was fighting 'em, huh? Flailing around with a piece of wood in his right hand, trying to shield himself with his left, isn't that what you said?"

"He still had the club in what the rats had left of his hand when they brought him in. Hanging on to it like it was going to save him. I saw it myself."

"Maybe that was his mistake, Lieutenant."

"What do you mean?"

"Well, if he'd concentrated on running—"

Lindgren shook his head. "The rats had it all figured out. He never had a chance."

"I can believe it," the boy said.

☐

Laddie went directly from the viewing procedure to the Center. He was too early to get into the information outlet, so he rode over to the boundary of ex-Hartford. Anybody who wanted to could go past the checkpoint and on in as far as a barrier. Beyond that only tours, conducted in safe vehicles, were allowed.

The buildings in this section of the city hadn't been tall, only three and four stories high. Some were rubble, others not. Laddie followed the prescribed route, marked by signs and double nets, until he came to the edge of the zone of higher buildings, where he could hear masonry falling off the rotting flanks of the skyscrapers, which were still losing hunks of their skin decades after they'd been abandoned. Warnings were up everywhere along the deserted streets. DANGER! BEWARE OF RATS. Laddie watched for a glimpse of one, or a scud of dust, but nothing moved—just as he'd guessed. Before he got to the barrier, he stopped, hid his bicycle behind a pile of rubble, and using stairs that were still sound, climbed to the second floor of a building, walked through it away from the street, scrambled back down to ground level, and made his way to the outer nets that guarded the inhabited area from the river. He followed the nets, which were anchored in concrete, toward an abandoned bridge. When he got to the approach to the bridge, which couldn't be seen from anywhere in the inhabited area, he discovered that the nets simply came to an end. He knew that rats were good swimmers, and that in the old days, they'd used sewers and other waterways to move from one area to another. *Yet the nets stopped!*

A rat could easily enter the inhabited area. The rat nets were a hoax. Probably the stories of rat invasions were lies. There were no packs of smart rats.

□

The information outlet was by then open. Laddie visited the new exhibition, which the librarian had told him about, where he found photographs of rat damage—examples of how they gnawed into granaries, chewed electric cords, even some cases of rat bite. Also there was scientific material on them—information about their mating habits and how they trained their young. There was also a rat skeleton.

Laddie studied the latter very carefully, especially the teeth, and concluded that the injuries inflicted on Joey couldn't have been done by rats, even assuming the packs of smart rats existed. Rats would have inflicted multiple small injuries, but Joey's mutilations had been different from that.

Add to that some other things. Joey had gone southeast, not north. Joey was left-handed—Laddie could visualize him holding up his left hand to make the Smart

Rats sign. Joey would never have held a club in his right hand. The story Lindgren had told was all a lie. If so, what *had* happened to Joey?

It was simple. He'd been butchered.

As Laddie left the museum, one of the caretakers was just putting up a big poster in the lobby, to reinforce the point of the new exhibition. It showed a group of teenagers, all of them horribly damaged in the same way Joey had been. They were tied upright against a rail. Some appeared to be dead already, some living. The caption underneath said:

DON'T RUN AWAY!
AN UNRATIONED LIFE ISN'T WORTH LIVING

☐

Barbara was in. She let Laddie come up to her apartment. He didn't look at it, couldn't have said afterward how big it was or what kind of furniture was in it. He hardly even looked at her. He paced back and forth while she watched him.

Then she made a guess. "Were you chosen for the progeny program? Is that it?"

"Boy, was I. By my own parents."

"When do you go?"

"October. But that's only the beginning."

"Tell me about it."

"I can't. I know too much that would be dangerous for you to know. But I can tell you what it's like to be me right now." Laddie stopped pacing and turned toward her, but he raised his eyes and looked over her head, like his mother when she was looking at trouble. "It's like I'm in this place somewhere and something's coming after me, and I'm boxed in and can't get away. The something, it's the system, and it's closing in on me, Barbara, and I can't do anything about it. And nobody else can, either. Nothing can make things turn out all right," he said. "Not this time. If I know anything, I know that. Nothing's ever right for people like us, only for the people who work for the Council. And when I think I might have been there!" He explained to her about his not applying for school.

Barbara said, "They have stones where their hearts should be. Believe me, I know."

"Then maybe that's what we should have."

"We can't, Laddie. We aren't put together that way. We can't act the way they do."

"I'd like the chance to try."

"I wouldn't like you then."

"Too bad. Would you like me better if I was crazy? Because I can tell you one thing, Barbara—if anything else goes wrong, I'll get as crazy as my younger sister."

"Is your younger sister crazy, Laddie?"

"That's one word for it—and that's part of it," he said. He went to the door. "I've got to move. I've got to keep moving. I may not get back again, Barbara. They're really closing in on me."

"Don't let them make you give up hope."

"There isn't any hope, not for me," Laddie said. "Except to join them, and it's too late for that."

He slammed the door and ran downstairs.

□

Laddie rode out of town, up and over the hill, and on beyond into the valleys, rode like a maniac, pedaled so recklessly that he fell twice and had a skinned knee and hand by the time he overtook Mrs. Vibert. She was out on the road, walking toward her house, carrying a large sunshade—she had the same fair skin as her son and daughter. She'd been at the Hernandez's, doing what she could for Joey's mother.

"Just look at your knee, Laddie. And your hand. You be sure you wash them both. Walk with me for a minute. What good luck that you came along like this so we can talk away from everybody. I have something I want to say to you. It's your sister. Your mother asked if she could play awhile with my Lily yesterday. I said she could, although—well, I don't really *like* to have Lily play with Greta. She told Lily things I know aren't true. She told Lily your father takes things from where he works and trades them."

"She—she told *Lily* that?"

"Yes, she did."

"You're right. It's not true."

"I know that. I don't know why she'd say it. Maybe she thinks it's a joke. Or maybe it's to get attention. But Laddie, if your sister will tell Lily that, she'll tell other people. You'd better stop her."

"Stop her?"

"*Stop* her," Mrs. Vibert said firmly. "You can't let her go on like that."

Laddie's hands dropped to his sides so his bike fell against him. He turned and stared at Mrs. Vibert.

"Are you all right, boy?"

"I— Yes, ma'am." He took hold of the bike again. "You're right. She's got to be stopped. And . . . thanks for telling me."

"I'd certainly want someone to tell me if Lily ever said anything like that about us."

"And you be sure to let me know when you hear from George again. If you do before I leave."

Laddie rode toward his house. Something else had just gone wrong, but he wasn't feeling crazy after all. His panic had faded. Instead, his mind was working. It had started to go again when he was talking to Mrs. Vibert. Linear. On target.

He had an achievable objective at last.

RATPOWER

16

Laddie lay awake, waiting for her to make her move. He heard a sound. Was it what he'd been waiting for? No. It was the wind outside.

He watched the moon rise. Nearly full, it cast bright cold light from his window onto the lower part of his bed. He had no covers over him. He'd left on his socks and briefs when he got undressed and put his sneakers beside the bed. That was all he'd wear. He didn't want to risk having wet clothes afterward. He tried to feel the moonlight on his bare legs. Couldn't. Wondered if there was anything about it that was measurable except its brightness. He wiggled his toes inside the socks, then curled them, as if he were trying to grip something with them. Some prey.

Another noise. Her door. Then Laddie heard just the slightest creak in the hallway, followed by a soft click. She was at it again. She'd been doing it every night during the past week. She'd learned that if she left after midnight, she could sneak out, as she had that first time, and nobody would discover it. She had been staying an hour or more, then coming back by the same outside stairs. Laddie hadn't tried to stop her, nor had he told his parents. He hadn't cared one way or the other what she did, but he'd been keeping track, mostly because he couldn't help it; he was next door.

He gave her plenty of time. Then he put on his sneakers and followed her.

The wind freshened his face and rumpled his hair. When he paused, it ran over his chest and belly and legs, gently, as if approaching him with love, or cleansing him—a ritual. The moonlight brightened the path and allowed him to keep well clear of the sourbush as he approached the bottom of the pond. Good. He didn't want scratches on his legs either.

She was out on the dam.

They'd had a thunderstorm the night before. There was plenty of spill.

He stepped onto the dam and went toward her. If he made any noise, the sound of falling water covered it.

She didn't notice him until he was almost up to her. She was so surprised to see him that she didn't move. She didn't have time to get angry or frightened—or prepared.

It was remarkably easy. The unpleasant part was the waiting, just to make sure.

17

"I think I'll get myself another mug of syntea," Arthur Grayson said. "You have to have something to wash down this new bread."

"Especially toasted," Louise said. "I'll get the tea. Do you want some more, Laddie?"

"Is there anything to wash the syntea down with?"

"Don't be so sassy." Louise smiled, then got a little teary. "It's just three weeks from today. Do you realize that?"

"Of course I realize it, Mom."

"How we're going to miss you!"

"Don't keep saying that," Arthur said. "He knows it

already and it doesn't help. I wonder where Greta is? She's always up by now."

"Let her sleep," Louise said.

"No." Arthur stood up. "I'm going to say good-bye to her. I think it's important for her to feel loved. I do think she behaves better when people make a fuss over her."

"Let her *sleep*," Louise said. "You wake her up. You leave the house. I'm stuck with her. What do you say, Laddie?"

"Me? No opinion."

A moment later Arthur gave a yelp. "She isn't here," he called. He ran downstairs. "Where can she have gone?"

"Where do you suppose?" Laddie said.

"The pond?" Laddie nodded. "She promised me she wouldn't ever go there again," Arthur said. "She must have got up before dawn. You didn't hear anything?" Laddie shook his head. "I'm going to make her promise to keep her promises from now on."

"She's never kept a promise in her life," Laddie said.

"Always after her, aren't you?"

"In three weeks I won't ever have to be after her again."

"Oh, don't remind me," Louise said. "I'd forgotten for a second."

"I never forget it, not even for a second," Laddie said.

"That's morbid," his father said. "Go get her. I don't have time."

Laddie leaned back in his chair. "Dad, one of the privileges I'm claiming in return for entering this progeny program is that I don't nursemaid Greta anymore. Hadn't you noticed?"

"I have to go to work," Arthur complained. "I don't need a demerit for tardiness, after all that's happened."

"Then let her stay at the pond until you get home this evening, unless Mom wants to go after her."

"Please don't bicker, you two. Art, you go and get her. Laddie shouldn't have to do things he doesn't want to do. You can pedal a little faster and still get to work on time."

"I hope she won't get mad at me," Arthur said. He hurried off in the direction of Bentham Pond.

Laddie estimated how many minutes it would take. His final guess was seven. In the event, it took closer to nine. His father didn't know the path all that well or exactly where to look when he got there.

□

"What a terrible thing to have happened. What a terrible thing to have happened," Arthur Grayson said. They were waiting for the mortuary team to come out from the Center. He looked at the clock. "You should have asked them when they'd get here, Laddie." Laddie had gone to the local provisions outlet beside the bus stop and had them radio the news in.

"I did ask them, Dad. I've told you that about five times."

"You should have asked them again. I wonder if one of us shouldn't go up and sit by the pond. Would you *mind* going up to the pond, Laddie? I don't suppose anything could happen to her, but it seems, well, nicer to have someone there. They'll want to talk to me. It's better if I stay here."

"What *could* happen to her?"

"She might float closer in to shore. You might be able to pull her out."

"I don't think anybody ought to touch her until the mortuary team gets here. It's their job. They ought to see exactly where she was when you found her and certify her condition and all the rest."

"There's no doubt about her condition. You don't have to be a mortuary team member to know about that. Oh, God!" Arthur groaned. "Poor little Greta."

"I wonder if she might have jumped in on purpose. She had this idea that she could swim if she wanted to."

"We'll never know. Go see how your mother is."

"I think we should leave her alone for a while."

Louise Grayson had had another collapse, like the one she'd had the day of the progeny program announcement. Laddie and his father had found her on the floor when they returned from the pond, where they'd gone to verify Arthur's first impressions before Laddie went to report the accident. They'd helped Louise upstairs and put her on the bed. They could hear her weeping now.

Laddie said, "What did you do with the brochure they gave you that first day, Dad? The one about the reduction program."

"It's in my dresser drawer, same as ever."

"I'll go get it."

"I thought you thought we shouldn't disturb your mother."

"I'll ask her how she is. Show her we care," Laddie said.

"Well, all right, but I don't see why you would want to look at a thing like that at a time like this."

Laddie brought the leaflet downstairs. "Read this fine print right here, Dad."

"I don't want to read anything right now."

"I'll read it to you. It's the footnote, remember? Bottom of page four. The exceptions. You don't have to hear them all, only this one." Laddie quoted. " 'If an unchosen progeny dies before the chosen progeny is picked up and taken away, the chosen progeny will be allowed to remain in place of the unchosen one, and that domestic unit will be considered to have only a single dependent progeny.' "

"How's that again? I'm having trouble concentrating, Laddie." Laddie reread it. "Does that mean you don't have to go away?"

"That's what it means," Laddie said.

"Good. We can use you here. Your mother's not all that well. She shouldn't be alone all day."

"I wonder if you shouldn't do something about it."

"Do something about what?"

"About my being excused from the program."

"Like what?"

"Well, maybe you have to make application."

"One thing at a time." There was a noise outside. "Here's the mortuary team. They must have left right after they got your message. Why couldn't they have told you they would?"

"Maybe they don't know so early in the morning how many customers they'll have that day."

□

After the funeral, Mrs. Vibert, carrying her sunshade, came up to speak to the family. She said how sorry she was, tears in her kindly eyes, then said to Laddie, "We've had another letter from George. So *soon* after the first one—it shows they aren't going to be all that strict, doesn't it? I brought it." She pulled an envelope out of her pocketbook. "I don't know if you'd want to look at it now."

"Of course I do." Laddie took the letter.

Dear Mom, Dear Dad, Dear Lily,
  Having a wonderful time. Wish you were here.
                                    Love, George

"Isn't that nice? Short and sweet," Mrs. Vibert said.

"And so like George. Not too original, just . . . nice."

"Yes, exactly." Mrs. Vibert put the letter away. "Losing your sister has surely been a great shock to you. People say they've heard Greta went all the time to that pond, even though she'd been given strict instructions not to. I know you shouldn't say anything about the dead, Laddie, but lies are lies, and now disobedience. Sometimes everything is for the best. It's not for us to question Providence, is it?"

"It certainly isn't," Laddie said.

☐

At lunch Arthur Grayson announced, "I'm going to say it one more time, and then that's it. I don't think we could have done anything to prevent it. That's what the meetingmistress said, and I think she's right. We couldn't keep Greta locked up, after all. If she insisted on escaping to that pond—well, what could we do?"

"Nothing, Art. Nothing," Louise said. All the grief had left her tired and irritable, and her limp was much worse because she'd had to stand so much and walk, too. "This is about the one hundredth time you've said you were going to say what you just said one more time and not say it again. This time I hope you mean it."

"Has it been so often?" Arthur said, frowning.

"You need something to get your mind off Greta," Laddie said. "You've got the rest of the day off, so why don't you go in to the Center and take care of applying for our exemption from the progeny program."

"Maybe it's automatic."

"Maybe it is. Only we don't know that. So I think you ought to go into the Center and make sure."

"I'd really prefer to let it take care of itself."

Laddie jumped to his feet. He slammed his hand down flat on the table. "For God's sake, use your head, Dad."

"Don't yell at your father. Laddie's right, Art."

"I suppose he is. It's just that—well, you don't know how it scares me to have anything to do with the government."

"In this case," Laddie said harshly, "there's a lot at stake. You were ready to send me away, so by God you'd better do what you have to to keep me."

"We had no choice," Louise said.

"Funny. I thought you did."

Louise looked out the window. "Do what he wants you to, Art."

Arthur went upstairs to get ready for the bike ride into the Center. Laddie stayed downstairs with his mother.

"Calm down, Laddie. Your father's in a state of shock. He loved Greta so. He was so excited to have a little girl. And remember how sweet she was when she was a tiny thing."

"I do remember that, Mom. But it's blotted out by . . . later."

"Thank God for you," Louise said. "It's like a miracle, to have you back."

"Mom, it's like two miracles. Two interconnected miracles. Because Greta would have brought this family down, sooner or later." Laddie told his mother what Greta had said to Lily Vibert.

Louise gasped, "No. Did she *really* say that to Lily?"

"Mrs. Vibert doesn't make things up, Mom. Greta was dangerous. I told you that."

"Is Mrs. Vibert safe? I mean, she won't repeat it, will she?"

"I don't think so." Laddie got up. "I'm going to the Center with Dad. I don't trust him. I want to make sure this gets done." He added, carefully, "And once I'm out of the program, I have some business of my own. With . . . the computer."

"Business of your own? Like what?"

"I'll tell you if it works out. It's got to do with my future. Now that I have a future again. Now that we all do. Think of that, Mom. *We all have a future again.*"

Louise looked up at Laddie. Gradually the expression on her face changed.

His own gaze was unwavering. "Mom, you look as if the other shoe just dropped."

She said slowly, "I think it just did." She raised a hand to her mouth. "Oh, my God," she whispered.

18

When they got to the administration building, Arthur Grayson balked. "Laddie, I just can't go in there." He pulled out a handkerchief and wiped the sweat off his forehead. "Look at me."

"You've *got* to go in."

"I can't. I can't." Arthur tried to bolt, but Laddie grabbed and held him. "I didn't tell you everything in front of your mother. That investigator, she said she wasn't closing the incident about the stapling machines. She said she was going to look into the whole operation at the distribution outlet. And she was looking at me all the time. I don't want to do *anything* to call attention to myself. You understand that, don't you? Why don't you go in and see if you can't do it for yourself."

"They're not going to take my word for all this. They'll need your disk. Probably they'll want your signature. I mean, why do I have to go on? It's all so obvious."

"I can't," Arthur said in a low voice. He tried to pull free.

Laddie got a better hold of him. "Here we go," he said roughly. He dragged Arthur up to the guard. "Get out your disk."

"What's the matter with him?" the guard said, suspiciously.

"It's my little sister. She just drowned. He has to come down here and straighten some things out. He's very upset."

The guard happened to have heard about Greta. He nodded and let them through.

It went quite easily. No red tape at all. Laddie's name was removed from the program and his appointment on the random pickup calendar canceled in a matter of seconds. Arthur wanted to go right home, and Laddie told him to go ahead and start out but to wait for him at the top of the hill beyond the Center, where Laddie would catch up with him.

Laddie then went to the computer terminal at the personnel outlet and disked in. When he got the initial menu, he typed 5 for "other."

WHAT OTHER SUBJECT DO YOU WANT TO
TAKE UP? (USE EXACT LANGUAGE. CONSULT
THE LIST OF ACCEPTABLE SUBJECTS ON THE
BULLETIN BOARD.)

Laddie had already consulted it. He typed COUNCIL
SCHOOL, PROCEDURES FOR APPLYING FOR.
The screen flickered.

YOU ARE ELIGIBLE FOR A COUNCIL SCHOOL.
DO YOU WISH TO APPLY TO ATTEND AT THIS
TIME? (Y/N)

Laddie gave it a Y. More blinking. Then:

YOU WILL BE NOTIFIED WHEN AND WHERE TO
GO FOR AN INTERVIEW. IF YOU HAVE NO FUR-
THER QUESTIONS, STRIKE "ENTER" TWICE.

Laddie struck ENTER twice, disked out, and went after
his father. As he passed Barbara's place, he saw her feet.
He stopped.

"Hey, Barbara. It's Laddie," he called. Her head
popped up. "I got saved from the progeny program. By
a miracle."

She pulled her robe up around her shoulders and
leaned over the balcony. "What kind of miracle?"

"I can't talk now. I'll come by again. Is that still okay?"

"Sure. Only I haven't changed type. Is *that* okay?"

"It'll have to be."

□

Arthur was resting beside his bike, looking dejected. "I didn't do so well down there, did I, Laddie? I've lost my nerve. That's what happens to you, after a while."

"Forget it, Dad." Laddie, too, got off his bike. "I guess you do as well as you can."

Arthur smiled at him, gratefully. "It's going to be a lot quieter now. Just the three of us out there in the country."

"Dad, I've just been at the personnel outlet. I've applied to go to a Council school."

Arthur thought it over. "We'd have to move?"

"I don't know. By the time I'm admitted, if I *am* admitted, I'll be eighteen, I expect. Technically, I'll be entitled to a place of my own."

"Well, if we have to move, I suppose we will. It'll be easier, now that we don't have Greta anymore." His father stopped. "It's like a new wound when I say something like that. You've *already* applied, you say?" Laddie nodded. Arthur shook his head slowly. "Think of it. A Council school. We'll be very proud of you, Laddie."

"It hasn't happened yet," Laddie said. "But if it does,

you and Mom will only have each other. I'm worried about her, Dad."

"There are so many things to worry about I hardly know where to start."

"True. There's something I found out I ought to tell you."

"If it's good news, go ahead. If it's bad, keep it to yourself, for right now." Arthur said.

"Fair enough. It's your choice. Let's get going. I'll tell you another time. Or maybe I won't . . . bother."

19

Less than a week after he'd made his application, Laddie was notified that a representative from NORSEC Center would be at Local Center 14 the following day. He should present himself at ten o'clock at the administration building. When he did so, he was sent to an office whose furniture was different from any he'd ever seen before: upholstered chairs placed for conversations, a clock ticking on a table, bookshelves. The massive old desk was of polished wood and had heavy brass fittings.

A short while later a man about fifty years old came in. He had on the uniform of a councilman, and over his shoulders a red hood, but no official hat. Laddie jumped to his feet.

"Sit down," the man said in a kindly way. He himself sat in a chair facing Laddie, rather than at the desk. He had papers in his hand. He put on heavy-rimmed glasses and read them through, carefully. Now and then he would raise his eyes and look at Laddie, then return to the papers. When he was finished, he said, "You have an interesting file, Arthur. I like what I find here. An active mind and some force to your character. I like that. Your immediate history is interesting, too. I see you were to be taken away in the progeny program, but . . . slipped through. To have been at risk in the first place was quite unnecessary. You are more than qualified to have attended a Council school. Ordinarily you'd have been rejected for school now because you've delayed so long, but some of us who have certain kinds of candidates in mind and don't want decisions being made routinely by computer—or the wrong people—review all new applications for school. That is why you're here today. Mind you, it may still be impossible. Can you tell me why you never applied before?"

Laddie had been watching the man closely and listening very carefully to what he said, looking for hints on what to say himself. He'd not overlooked the phrases "slipped through" and "at risk." Hardly the official line. It suggested a guarded candor might be in order.

"I didn't apply because my family brought pressure on me not to, sir."

"I assumed it must have been something like that. Why did they do so?"

"Because of my younger sister."

"The girl who drowned. She has a puzzling file. I have your entire family here in my hands, you see." The man touched his papers. "Before she was taken out of school, several of her teachers commented on her. Then—let's see—she was needed at home, it says, after your mother had a fall several years ago. She was never sent back to school after that. They never called her back, either—of course they're only too glad to get rid of a pupil when they can. Hmm. No follow-up—I mean to the doubtful teachers' reports. If she'd stayed in school, I suspect there'd have been tests called for by this time." The man's face was expressionless now, neither inviting nor declining a confidence. "I suppose your mother and father wanted to keep her out of sight."

Laddie pushed forward. "That's what it came down to. And if I'd applied, we'd have had to move to a center while I was in Lower School. More people would have noticed Greta."

"Well, that's all over now. Curious, about her drowning. Tell me about it."

Laddie repeated the story he and his father had given the morning of Greta's death. When he'd finished, the man simply said, "Lucky for you. Now tell me, how did you feel about the progeny program?"

"Can I be honest?" The man nodded, and Laddie bet all on his next answer. "I thought of it as a death sentence."

"Did you?" The man took off his glasses, then replaced them. "*Did* you! Why?"

"If things are so bad here, think what they must be like in regions that had to be abandoned."

"Mmm. Quite. And what do you think of your life in general? Here, where things, as you say, are so bad."

"Not much."

"Elaborate on that."

"I have a mother who's maybe not all that well, and a father who's lost his nerve."

"You haven't lost yours, I have to say."

"Don't think I don't realize this is my only chance. I mean right now, talking to you. If I don't get across to you—"

"Go on about your life."

"I haven't been able to get work since I stopped school. I've got a hunch when I do get work it'll be dangerous. I'm hungry a lot of the time, like everybody else. Cold in the winter, like them. Not much education, and what I had wasn't much good."

"No reason to cheer so far," the man said dryly.

"Is there any reason I *should* like my life?"

"I'd be hard pressed to provide you with one. Is there nothing in your life that pleases you?"

"I used to have three good friends who lived near me. They helped. I really liked them, especially two of them. One of them was taken away not long ago, along with his family, on a Trade and Barter charge. They'd . . . confessed. My friend could hardly walk at the deportation procedures. He'd been tortured; you could see it. They used an electric prod on him. He screamed, sir. My friend screamed. My second friend was taken away in the progeny program. The third friend ran away and was captured and brought around as an exhibit. We all had to go see him. He was cut to pieces. Blind. Tongue gone. Tendons chopped. They said it was done by a pack of smart rats. He tried to defend himself, they said. With a club. They said he was flailing it around with his right hand, trying to defend himself, that's exactly what they said. They were very particular about it. With his right hand. I don't understand that, sir. My friend was about as left-handed as anyone I've ever known. I did a little research on rats. Saw pictures of rat-bite victims. Looked at skeletons, especially at the teeth. I'd say the damage done to my friend couldn't have been done by rats. Of course I may be wrong."

"Have you a theory about what did happen to your friend?"

Laddie didn't reply to the question directly. "I've been thinking that I live under a certain system. It's not going to change. If you live under a system, it's better to be on the inside than on the outside of it. Isn't that so?"

"Let's return to your friends. Do you miss them?"

"All the time, sir. Especially Sam, the one who was deported. If I could have any wish I wanted, I guess my first one would be to go to a Council school. If I had a second wish, it would be that Sam could go with me."

The man looked very seriously at Laddie. "Something that was missing before is now there."

"What do you mean?"

"I'm not interested in a boy who's merely ambitious, Arthur. They're easy to find. Let us get on. I should explain that I am a member of the governing committee of the College of Scientists. Also, as it happens, I'm a councilman. It puts me rather . . . beyond the reach of many people." The man sat thinking for several minutes. He made a note or two to himself, then went to the computer terminal that sat on the desk. It took him a few minutes to make connection, then he keyboarded, waited, keyboarded again, waited, finally keyboarded one last time. "It could be worse," he said as he returned to his chair. "This progeny program has thrown recruitment procedures off, as some of us predicted would happen from the beginning. That being the case, regular procedures *can*, with due cause, be modified. But you are too old to go to Lower School. You'll have to go directly to Upper School."

"Won't I be behind the other students?"

"They waste a lot of time the first couple of years, but, yes, you will be. And you're not in Upper School yet. Here is what you must do. I will have you sent a package of textbooks and sample questions. You must study. Harder than you've ever done anything in your life. Work fifteen hours a day, every day, from now until mid-December. You will then be given a written examination. It will be only slightly modified from the exam others take after two years of school. It will be computer graded, and you *must* pass it. You will also have an interview. If you are certified, you will then enter the Upper School, but on a modified course of studies for the first six months, after which you will join the regular Upper School classes. Is that all clear?"

"Yes, sir."

"Go home and wait for the books. They'll be at your house within twenty-four hours."

The man shook Laddie's hand—the first time any nonrationed person had ever touched him. "I am rather . . . extending myself on your behalf. I expect a lot from you."

"Don't worry." Laddie stopped at the door. "Sir, I have one thing I'd like to ask. A favor." He explained about his father and his troubles at work. "All over nothing. They found the stapling machines. But he thinks he's in trouble, and he may be right. The investigator cited some other very small errors in his record. I won't even bother to tell you about them. I don't want to have to worry about him while I'm studying."

"I'll put a block on his file."

"And my mother, sir?"

"On hers, too. Indefinitely. Should something go wrong, tell the investigator or whoever to get in touch with Councilman Weaver at the College of Scientists before taking any action."

Laddie said, with a shake of his head, "It's that easy?"

Councilman Weaver nodded. "If you have power."

☐

Laddie stopped at Barbara's place.

This time he looked around at her apartment, while she made them glasses of synthade. She had one room and a tiny kitchenette, plus the balcony. A daybed that had pillows piled up on it where she slept, a few straight chairs and one comfortable one, sheets of paper pinned to the walls, on which she'd drawn pictures. One of them was of her own feet up on the balcony. It made him smile. Life seen from an odd angle.

He asked her some questions about herself. She worked in the battery factory, but only irregularly. She might not be able to keep the apartment, as things were going. She'd had a regular job before her friend's deportation.

Laddie carried two of the chairs onto the balcony. "Let's put our feet up on the railing," he said, "the way you were that first day. Okay?" When they'd done so, he said, "Your toes are *almost* touching the toes of a guy who's going to Council school. Maybe."

She turned in her chair without moving her feet. "You? A Council school?" She gave him a funny look. "What are you doing here, in that case?"

"Why not?"

"People like me don't know people like you."

"They do if people like me want it that way." He described what had happened. "I'll be studying my tail off, but I'll have to take breaks. I'd like to take them here. With you."

"Same conditions."

"Maybe I could touch your toes with mine once in a while?"

"I don't think so."

Laddie turned in the way she had, without moving his feet. "There isn't anyone else left I can talk to."

"I miss my friend," she said.

"And you've got beautiful gray eyes. And shoulders."

"That's enough of that."

As he was leaving, Laddie remembered to ask her about her sister and her children. Barbara said they were all right for a few years. The progeny program didn't take kids under seven, and the oldest of her sister's children was only four. "Though it's always possible they'll change the rules. If they don't, maybe by the time the oldest one is old enough to go, the program will be canceled."

"Or maybe by that time I can do something for them." Laddie told Barbara what Councilman Weaver had done for his mother and father. "Just like that." Laddie doubled up a fist. "If you've got the power, you can do just about anything."

Barbara looked at the fist, then at his face, and said, "Can you have the power without turning into one of them? That's something to think about." She added, "When you're not studying."

20

Laddie passed the written examination with distinction. Councilman Weaver himself came to Local Center 14 to give the oral examination on December 23rd.

"You pass, Arthur. Congratulations," he said when it was over. "Now you'll have your six-month special stint, then take general courses for a year. After that you'll specialize. Should you choose science, you'll encounter me again. I teach occasionally in the Upper Science School. In the meantime, I'll be keeping an eye on you."

Laddie was told to report to Local Center 14 on January 2nd, for transportation to NORSEC Center to begin his formal schooling. A clerk took his rationed citizen's disk and issued him temporary identification, countersigned by Councilman Weaver, that said he was a student in the Upper School and under its special jurisdiction. He was also issued a uniform, so he wouldn't have to report in the shabby clothes of a rationed citizen.

☐

He was at loose ends on New Year's Day, the main holiday of the year in NORSEC. He didn't want to stay home. It hadn't been so bad as long as he had his cramming to do, but now that that was finished, he was bothered by the way his mother acted toward him. Distant. Almost fearful.

He'd lost her. One day he might talk to her about it, and she might come to understand. In the meantime, he didn't intend to let her make him feel doubts about himself.

The weather was mild. NORSEC had only small amounts of snow since the climate had changed, and had none at all on the ground this year. Laddie took a bicycle and went around his own mile, past the houses where Joey and George had lived, then to Sam Pratt's house. He got off his bike and went to the shed where the Smart Rats had held their meetings. He stayed there a few minutes, thinking of his friends.

When he was about to leave the shed, he made the Smart Rats sign and said aloud to the ghosts, "I'll remember, guys." It struck him as false. There were so many other things to think about now.

He went outside to his bicycle and rode on. Inevitably, he ended up walking his bike to the pond.

The trees had lost their leaves and the glo-cards on them were bright in the winter sun, except for one that had fallen off and was caught in the brush. Laddie, without thinking about it, reattached it to the tree, where it legally belonged; he was affiliated to the Council now. There was not much ice around the water's edge. Not much water, either. Winter was such a dry season that the level was very low. He went out on the dam, for the first time since that moonlit night. Thoughts about Greta, which came to him often enough, led him to his usual conclusion. He'd done the right thing.

He returned to the road, went home and changed into his new uniform, then went to the Center, where Barbara was expecting him. She'd been away for a week, to see her sister, and had come back just that morning. He'd told her before she left that he wanted to spend part of this afternoon with her—the last of the many visits he'd paid her—and she'd returned a day early. It gave Laddie hopes.

She opened her door, frowned when she saw how he was dressed, and stepped back away from him as he came forward. She touched the rich blue cloth of his sleeve. "My, my." She read his new identification certificate, which he took out of his pocket. "You're moving up there," she said, mockingly. "My, *my*. Arthur Ladd Grayson 'under the special jurisdiction of the Council and not subject to those in authority over rationed citizens.' *My*, my."

"Yeah, I am moving up," Laddie said. He knew he looked good in his uniform, and he felt good in it, too. There was no cause for her to make fun of him, and he didn't like it. He sat down and tilted back his chair. "Maybe that'll change your mind. About 'conditions.' "

"Just the opposite."

"And it doesn't matter that I'm leaving tomorrow?"

"It matters."

"I like you a lot."

"I like *you* a lot."

He began to get angry. He hadn't been sleeping. He was depressed about his mother. He was worried about what was coming. "I've been as nice as I knew how with you, Barbara. Kept my distance. Don't think I haven't wanted to . . . press you every time I've been here. I've always hoped that sooner or later we'd make out. I don't see why we haven't, and I don't see why you won't now." He tipped forward and doubled up his fists and put one on each knee. "It's stupid. We see each other like this, talk about everything, really get to know each other well, and yet you won't make love. It's *really* stupid. I don't know whether to have hurt feelings or throw something or both."

"Come on, Laddie." She sat on a stool in front of him, took each of his hands in turn, and made him relax his fists. "The last thing I mean to do is hurt your feelings."

He stood up. "There are other reasons why you ought to cooperate," he said, standing over her.

"You see making love as a form of cooperation?"

"Don't twist what I say. I'll have connections, Barbara. And I'll have the power we talked about. I can do you favors."

"What if I don't want your favors?"

He scowled at her. "I could also be dangerous," he said.

"Are you serious?"

"I'm just pointing things out."

"Poor you."

"What does that mean?"

"It means I think maybe you'd better go away." Barbara, too, stood up.

He took her shoulders in his hands. "I could use a send-off. Please." He smiled. "You don't seem to like my new uniform. I'll have to get out of it if we make love." He tried to draw her closer, but she resisted.

"Laddie, you won't ever be able to spend any time with me again, you realize that? They won't allow it. You'll be whatever you are, I'll still be rationed. To make love with you, for me, is a real dead end. I'll only be sorry."

"But you would otherwise, you mean? Would, if I were stuck in the same lousy world you are?"

"I mean that your new rank is an additional reason not to do what you want."

"And what are the original reasons? I don't think I've ever known them."

Barbara looked at him, as if unsure how far she could go. "I'm still mourning for my friend Pete, I suppose that's part of it. And Laddie, something about you worries me. It has ever since you went for that interview. Let's say that you've left me behind and leave it at that."

"This is a pretty big day in my life. I hadn't expected to lose you."

"Thanks for coming in to see me, Laddie. And I mean it when I say thanks for wanting to make love. And you *know* I mean it when I wish you good luck."

"Could I have that drawing of your feet? As a souvenir?" Barbara nodded and took it off the wall and rolled it up and tied it with a piece of string. Laddie touched it to his lips. "Close as I'll ever get, right?" He held it carefully. "If I hadn't come like this, dressed like this, would you—?"

"You'll never know. You'll know more and more, when you go to your school, but you'll never know that," Barbara replied.

"*You* know I didn't mean what I said about being dangerous."

"Yes, I know. But we mustn't, either one of us, forget that it's true. Good-bye, Laddie."

Laddie had never felt more lonely than he did as he left Barbara's apartment, but he reminded himself, once he was outside, that he was on his way tomorrow and would never be back. That helped.

21

Laddie placed at the top of his class in the special course of studies and was moved on into the regular course at the end of June. A year later, he took qualifying examinations and placed at the top in them. He had his choice of tracks at that time: He could continue with general work in preparation for a career in the administration; he could take the military track and train as an officer in the several Law Enforcement Corps; he could prepare himself as a statistician, psychologist, or sociologist; or he could take the science track. He chose the latter.

There was a graduation ceremony. His mother and father couldn't be present since they were not admitted inside NORSEC Center, but Councilman Weaver came and sat in the audience. The principal's commencement address was the same one he gave each year, suitable for students who were now surely on their way toward rank. He began by reminding them that they were the survivors in a selection process that had begun in Lower School and continued here in Upper School.

"Those who didn't measure up have been remanded to rationed life, but you measured up, and so you are entering a new phase of your careers."

Next the principal reminded them of how, after the troubles of the first half of the century, "strong and determined men and women joined forces and created the system of conciliar government on this continent and throughout the world. What is the purpose of the system and its rationale? Nothing less than to preserve civilization and at the same time try to overcome the fateful legacy of the past, when the planet Earth was so irreparably damaged. You will soon become a part of the system. Yours will be a heavy burden.

"In return—" The principal raised his head. "In return, you will have privileges."

He paused so long some of the students shifted uneasily in their chairs.

"Let me address the ethics of privilege.

"There was a joke that used to get passed around here in NORSEC Center. 'Question: What's the unwritten law of NORSEC? Answer: When there isn't enough to go around, the strong take what they want and the weak get what's left.' "

More shifting in chairs.

"You're surprised. Shocked. As I mean that you should be. But I haven't finished."

The principal walked over to a blackboard and wrote an equation.

WHEN THERE ISN'T ENOUGH TO GO AROUND

$$\frac{\text{THE STRONG TAKE WHAT THEY WANT}}{} = \text{DUTY \& RESPONSIBILITY}$$

AND THE WEAK GET WHAT'S LEFT!

"Think about that a moment."

After another pause, he continued. "On the one hand, you, as the strong, will have your privileges. But in return, you will be responsible for the survival of civilization. Your privileges will be the recompense you receive in return for shouldering that responsibility. I want all of you to think of your time here not as a preparation for the enjoyment of privileges, but as preparation for the execution of your duties.

"Go forth from this school now and prosper, in the name of the president and Council of NORSEC."

The students rose and responded, "To whom be all

honor and obedience," then broke into cheers and applause.

Laddie's classmates fell back out of respect for conciliar rank when Councilman Weaver came up to shake his hand.

"Do you know what humbug is, Arthur?" Laddie shook his head. "You've just had it defined by example. Come. We'll have dinner together."

As they were eating, Weaver said, "I would like to tell you what some of us are doing—botanists, biologists, and so forth—to try to alleviate the difficulties of life. You recall that you told me about your friends. We can't bring them back, but we can try to help others like them. That's not a bad objective, Arthur. A better one than the one you just heard at your graduation ceremony. I hope you will one day share it with us."

"I'd be honored to, sir."

"Do you still think about your friends?"

"Less than before. I've been pretty busy."

"Don't forget them. Or your family. Sometimes, under our system, it's hard to remain human, Arthur. Memory helps, if we cultivate it."

"Yes, sir. Sir, couldn't you call me Laddie? Everybody always has."

Weaver shook his head. "It won't do here," he said. "Not yet, at any rate."

22

The Upper Science School occupied several of the buildings that had once been part of a university located in the town where the Council of NORSEC had its main center. Laddie lived in one of the dormitories, which had a number of entrances; one, on the ground floor, was a room designated the office. A student was on duty there at night, and the other students were obliged to sign in and out if they wanted to go off to eat or exercise or socialize at one of the places open to students, but nobody kept close tabs on them. It was assumed they would take care of themselves.

On Monday of his second week in science school, Laddie got up at six o'clock in the morning to go running.

He turned left and went for half a mile, past a park, then started up a broad, shady avenue, where trees, survivors from long ago, were kept healthy by the application of special chemicals and sprays. He passed another jogger, who was coming from the opposite direction.

Laddie stopped, looked back, turned around, and followed the young man, slowly closing the distance between them until he was only fifteen feet in the rear. When they reached a big house, now turned into apartments, the other jogger slowed and started up the front stairs to a broad porch. Satisfied that he knew where the man lived, Laddie trotted on by him as the man bent to stretch his legs and back.

Laddie returned to the office and signed in, went to his own entrance and room, showered, and went off to breakfast with his roommate, an exchange student from SOUWESEC, where the science school was weak. Laddie was preoccupied and didn't eat as much as usual, though he'd just been exercising. The chance encounter in the avenue had revived an old objective.

☐

"Ready to go, Lieutenant Lindgren?"

"Yep. Feel like a long one, Art?" Lindgren asked, as he put a sweatband around his blond hair.

"I'll go it as long as you do. You choose where. You know the good routes."

"We're off, then." Lindgren set the pace, his new student friend, Arthur Grayson, right at his side.

Arthur was deferential. This morning he asked Lindgren about his work.

"I've been second in command of Confession Procedures. Training corpsmen. Supervising them when they practice. That sort of thing," Lindgren said.

"Practice what?"

"Confession Procedures."

"Who do you practice on?"

"Whoever they give us."

"Is it difficult work?"

"Not very. You know from the outset what you want to make them say, and you make them say it. The only interest about Confession Procedures is in being creative in your methods. However, I've just been given new duty. Let's take a left turn here, okay? It's an extension of yesterday's route. I'm now in charge of the servile barracks. They don't like to keep an officer on confessions too long. This new assignment is considered an advancement."

They jogged on until they'd come a circle. It was their fourth run together, in as many days. On Tuesday Arthur had come by just as Lindgren was starting out and asked if he could join up, said he was new at it and didn't know the good routes. They'd made it a regular thing for the rest of the week.

When they stopped, Lindgren checked his watch, an elaborate one with stopwatch and calculating features, to see what their timing and speed had been.

Arthur was impressed by it. "That's what I call a real watch."

"Nice, isn't it? Actually, I have two of them."

"*Two* of them!"

"You ought always to have a backup of a thing like this." Lindgren smiled. "Of course you can't get two just by asking. Or even one. Damned shortages. These were left over from a deportation demonstration I ran a year or two ago. Trade and Barter case. I got watches issued to me for the evidence, and this guy"—Lindgren tapped his wrist—"and the backup just didn't happen to get turned back in afterward." He slipped the watch off his wrist. "Take it. A loan."

"That's really nice of you." Arthur removed the simple model they issued students and put the new one on.

"A loan for as long as we run together," Lindgren said.

"Then we'll be running together a long time if I get my way," Arthur said.

"You drink?" Lindgren asked.

"I've had some beers."

"Let's have a few together tonight, if you want to. It's Friday."

"I have classes tomorrow."

"I'm not asking you to stay out all night. I'll meet you at the beverage outlet on the other side of the park, opposite those pools. Ten o'clock. If you get there first, tell them I'm coming. That outlet isn't open to students unless they're accompanied."

☐

Lindgren was already drunk when he got to the outlet, where Arthur was waiting. He'd just had a big blow, he said. He'd only found out that afternoon. He'd been passed over for promotion again. He'd expected to make captain last year but hadn't made it. Now he hadn't made it this year, either. It wasn't fair. Someone was really screwing him.

"I'm drunk, and I'm going to get drunker and then I'm going to the servile barracks and help myself to a girl. Get laid, by God. You can come along. Take your pick."

"Where are the servile barracks, Lieutenant?"

"All over. The one I want is just beyond your school."

"Are there a lot of girls in the barracks?"

"We'd have a lot more, and some real nice young ones, if they'd put the goddamned progeny program on servile-recruitment status. A lot of choice stuff going off in that who'd grab at servile status, given the alternative."

"What *is* the alternative, sir?"

Lindgren looked woozily at Arthur. "You'll be told when it's time. Anyway, that program's off-limits. I think it's stupid, because we're always short of serviles, but I'm not calling the shots. So how about it? You itching for a blonde or a brunette? I might even be able to find you a virgin. Let you at her first, just this once. You like that idea?"

"I like the *idea*, but . . . I'm doing okay as it is."

"Yeah?" Lindgren was interested. "You making out with another student, Arthur?"

"Let's say I'm working on it."

"I'd like to meet her."

"You think I'd risk that?"

Lindgren grinned. "I promise I'll be good. Let's have another."

□

About eleven thirty, Lindgren had a conversation with the bartender, an elderly servile so trusty she was allowed to sleep on the premises.

"How many of these do you think I can drink before closing time, Della?"

Della estimated five.

"Line them up right now."

"I'm going to have to go, Lieutenant," Arthur said.

"Saturday classes—a pain in the ass. I'll see you on Monday. We'll go a new route."

"Great. Take good care of this guy, Della."

☐

After he'd signed in at the office, where his roommate was on duty until four A.M., Laddie went up to his bedroom. He undressed and lay down on his bed and looked at the ceiling, calculating the risks. Later, he thought to look out the window. Not as much of a moon as the other time.

A little before one, he got up and put on his running clothes and left the dormitory. All the lights were out except for the one in the office, across the dark courtyard. He trotted into the empty park and proceeded to the shallow ornamental pools that were directly on the line Lindgren would take when he went to the servile barracks after the beverage outlet closed at one o'clock.

Low signs were set in the ground at the edge of the pool. DO NOT WADE—WATER CONTAINS ANTI-POLLUTANTS. Fingers drumming his thighs now, tense and excited, Laddie estimated how a person, say a drunk, who tripped over one of the signs, might fall.

That part was okay. He checked the time, then removed his new watch, lest it glitter, and put it in the little pocket just below the drawstring of his shorts. He looked around. Nobody in sight. Then he concealed himself in the shrubbery.

A few minutes after one, Lyman Lindgren, his officer's cap on at a jaunty angle, came through the door of the outlet with Della, who walked him across the street. Some other customers came out, watched, laughed, and yelled. Lindgren waved an arm. Della aimed Lindgren toward the walk.

He staggered forward. The other customers cheered him on, then went off in the opposite direction. He veered from the walk and bumped into a tree and stopped to get his bearings. Della called to ask him if he wanted a patrol car to take him home, but he yelled no. She went inside and turned off the front lights. Lindgren staggered on. When he came to the first pool, he stopped and looked down, weaving on his feet.

Laddie stepped up behind him. His lips formed a word:

RATPOWER!